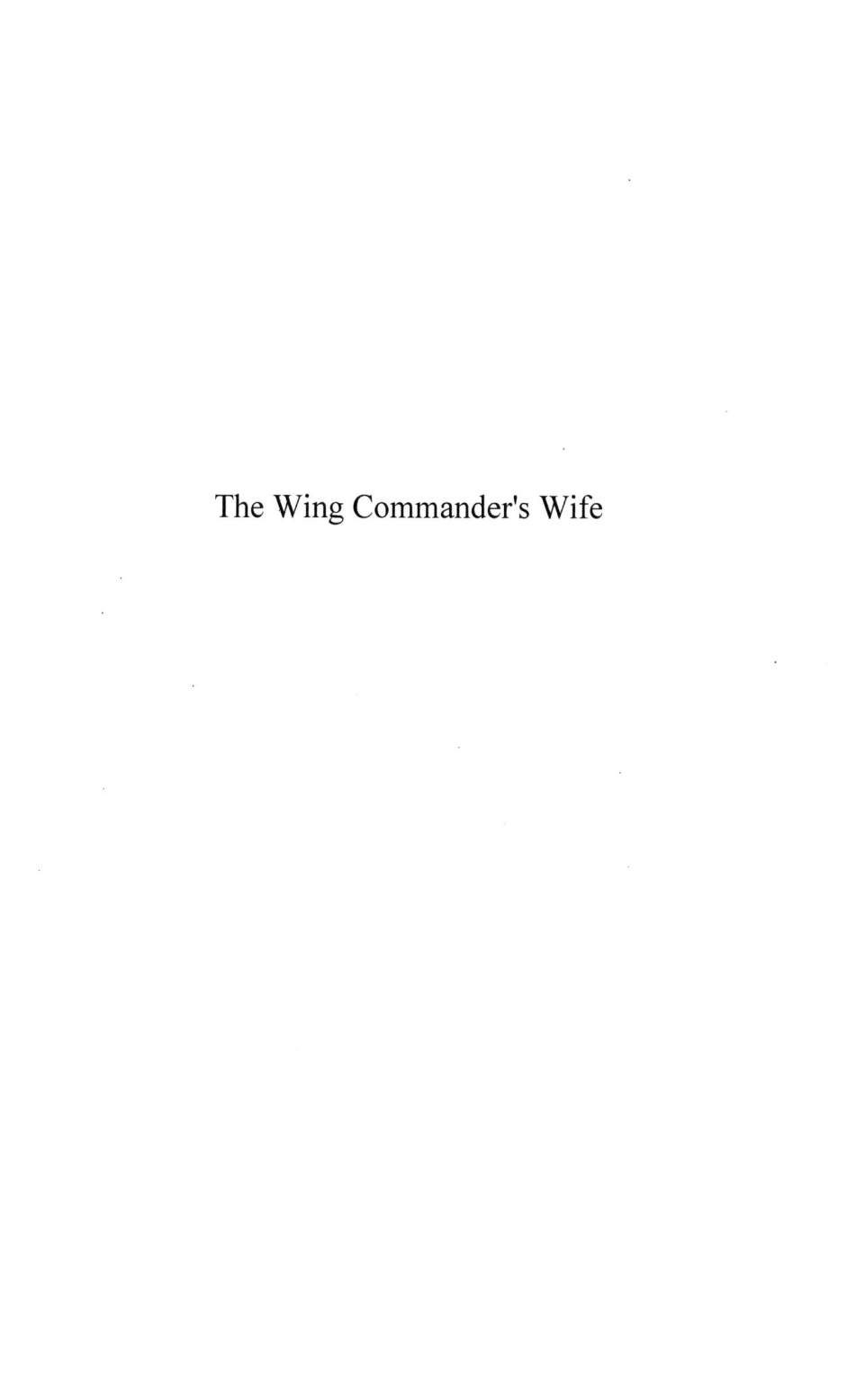

The Wing Commander's Wife

About the author

W Stephen Beakhouse was born in 1927. Considered to be a 'naughty' child, it was Wallace's mother who first realised that something was wrong. Diagnosed with a mental health disability; the author battled through school and went to work in the coalmines, before ending his career as a bus driver. W Stephen Beakhouse now lives in Reading.

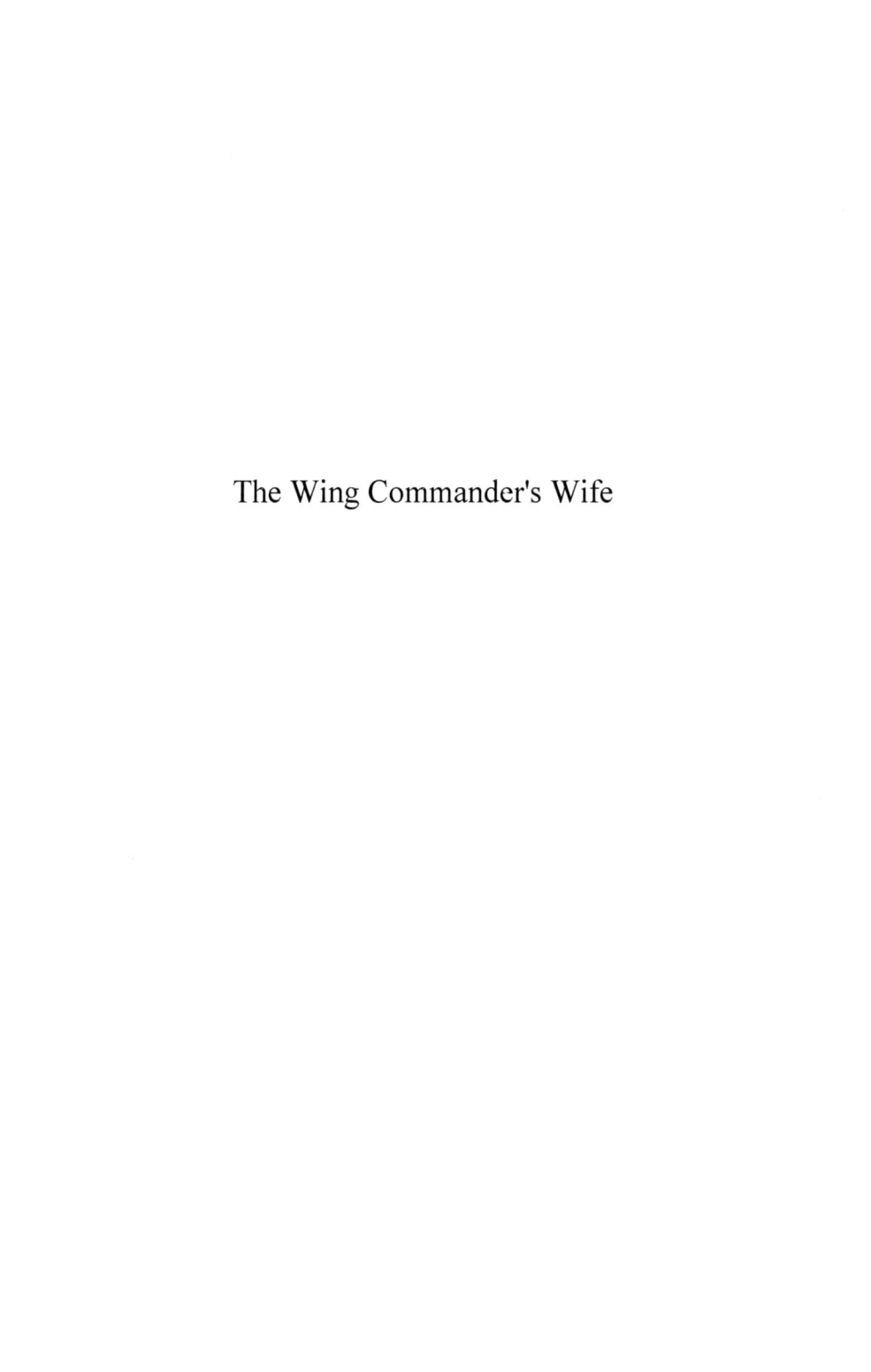

The Wing Commander's Wife

W Stephen Beakhouse

The Wing Commander's Wife

Olympia Publishers
London

www.olympiapublishers.com
OLYMPIA PAPERBACK EDITION

Copyright © W Stephen Beakhouse 2013

The right of W Stephen Beakhouse to be identified as author of
this work has been asserted in accordance with sections 77 and 78 of the
Copyright, Designs and Patents Act 1988.

All Rights Reserved

No reproduction, copy or transmission of this publication
may be made without written permission.
No paragraph of this publication may be reproduced,
copied or transmitted save with the written permission of the publisher, or
in accordance with the provisions
of the Copyright Act 1988 (as amended).

Any person who commits any unauthorised act in relation to
this publication may be liable to criminal
prosecution and civil claims for damage.

A CIP catalogue record for this title is
available from the British Library.

ISBN: 978-1-84897-305-3

(Olympia Publishers is part of Ashwell Publishing Ltd)

This is a work of fiction.
Names, characters, places and incidents originate from the writer's
imagination. Any resemblance to actual persons, living or dead is purely
coincidental.

First Published in 2013

Olympia Publishers
60 Cannon Street
London
EC4N 6NP

Printed in Great Britain

CHAPTER 1

From Mr Jones' office he presented himself at RAF Maggadore's HQ and informed the Sergeant-in-charge of his new duty and the reason for his presence. The process of rank then began. The Sergeant informed Wing Commander Churton's PA that Aircraftsman F.W. Radnor was there to be interviewed by the Wing Commander. FW was marched into his office. He saluted and was told to stand at ease. In a light-hearted way the Wing Commander said that he hoped that:
"You, Aircraftsman, will last longer than your predecessors," and added, "When is your demob due?"
FW replied, "About two to three years, sir."
"Good, let's hope we get along. I would like to introduce you to my wife, but at the moment she is away. You have your instructions, haven't you?"
"Yes, sir. I report to you or your office every day unless instructed otherwise at 08.00 hours."
"That's correct. I don't require you today but perhaps tomorrow. I'm not sure. That will be all."
The day came when the Wing Commander's wife needed the car to take her to the NAAFI store and to call for her at 09.00 hours. He drew up outside the villa and went to say that her car was there. She emerged from the front door, but he doubled back to the car and waited for her, holding the rear passenger door open for her to enter. What he saw coming towards him was the most beautiful

and attractive lady he had seen in his life. She had long, blonde hair down to her shoulders, her face made up to perfection, with a perfect figure and a walk which defied description. In fact, for a second he thought she was a mirage. As she got near to the car he saluted her and stuttered:

"Good morning Madam."

She had not noticed him – to her he was just another driver. She tartly told him he did not have to salute her. He then at once put out his right hand to shake hers. By this unexpected gesture she was taken aback and reluctantly offered her netted, gloved hand in return. Next to arrive at the car was the Indian housekeeper and she responded with a "Thank you Sahib. We would like to go to the NAAFI stores."

"Yes, of course. I have driven some NCOs' wives there but not in a Humber Snipe before."

Neither of these two people imagined what fate had in store for them.

Arriving at the NAAFI stores provided for officers' wives, Mrs Churton did not make any attempt to get out of the car, sitting in the back alone. She looked down in the dumps. He asked her if there anything was wrong.

"No not really," she replied, "I just don't like going in there. They all look and talk about me."

She gave the housekeeper a shopping list and further instructions that if there were any problems she should come out to the car but that there should not be any.

"Very good ma'm sab, I understand."

Freddie was already outside the car. Mrs Churton remained in her seat looking sorry for herself.

"Do you mind if I have a cigarette Madam? Perhaps you would like one – that is if you smoke?"

"Driver, that is the best offer I have had for some time thank you. I will come out and join you."

She was fiddling about to find her own cigarettes when he said, "Here have one of mine."

There was a slight breeze and as she cupped her hands around his to light up, her eyes looked up at this tall young airman who had entered her life, neither of them realized what had begun.

All went well and when they got back to the villa the second sign, albeit a very small one, appeared. She thanked him, shook his hand and said:

"I feel much better now – I am going to have a stiff drink and a sleep."

CHAPTER 2

Two weeks had passed since their first meeting. Freddie took the Wing Commander to official duties and various social engagements. On one occasion, the Commander commented:

"Thank you Aircraftsman, I won't be needing you tomorrow, but my wife will. Together with Flt. Lt. Elison's wife they are both going to a big charity function about 25 miles from the base. If you don't know where it is, my wife will show you."

"Very good sir," he saluted and withdrew. Next day, as arranged, Freddie called for Mrs Churton. He then drove to the married quarters and called for Mrs Elison. Again, he shook hands with his new passenger. Both of them sat in the back as normal. But, to his surprise, there was no small talk between them. Freddie had no difficulty in locating the venue. It was a grand-looking building and in the car park there were a number of large cars so it was obviously an important occasion. About mid-afternoon they both emerged to be taken home. Freddie enquired as a matter of courtesy whether they had had a successful day. Both responded that they had. Off he drove them and went towards base. The car had gone about three miles when Mrs Churton shouted over to Freddie:

"Driver stop the car, I am going to be sick."

Freddie pulled off the road onto a dry dusty patch but it was too late. Mrs Churton was vomiting over everything.

Mrs Elison shouted in anger at Mrs Churton.

"Really Deborah, you're the bloody limit. Why do you drink so much? You know you can't take it." She got out of the car and stormed off. Freddie went to Mrs Churton's aid. She looked terrible and cascading all down her front was vomit. He managed to get her out of the car. She was limp and crying. Freddie propped her up against the side of the car and reached for anything to mop some of the vomit off of her. He used everything he had as he dried her front. All she had on was a floral dress which was wet through. It outlined her beautiful breasts and his hand passed over them as he was trying to dry her. As he did, he was suddenly sexually aroused. He had never been so close to a woman before but, when he realized what was happening, the feeling soon went away.

"Mrs Churton, Deborah! Can you hear me? Please say something, or even nod."

She then spluttered out, "Yes."

Freddie then said, "I must get you to the base hospital without delay. Please, Madam, if I help you can you sit in the front seat next to me. You can't sit in the rear as it is a mess." He got her into the car. These Humber Snipes had one long bench seat in the front.

He asked her, "Are you alright?"

She mumbled, "Get me home quickly please."

"Yes, but I must find Mrs Elison first."

"Bugger Mrs Elison, leave her."

"Well, I would like to but I am responsible for you both." With that Mrs Elison appeared and she too had been sick. She said to Deborah:

"I'm sorry I shouted at you Deborah, I do apologize. I'm sure we've both got food poisoning or something."

Freddie said, "Hurry and get in Mrs Elison, I must get you both to the station hospital."

Both were seated in the front as the back seats were in a disgusting state. There was plenty of room in the front seat for three. Mrs Churton was very close to Freddie and the vomit down her front began to smell, even with the windows wound down.

Freddie was driving as fast as he could. About three miles from the base he felt Mrs Churton's arm between the back of his part of the seat and the middle of his back and her head was limp on his shoulder. In a way it was nice, spoilt only by the smell. Mrs Elison did not speak a word.

CHAPTER 3

He drove into the grounds of the Officers' Hospital with the horn sounding. At the main entrance Freddie got out and rushed inside to raise the alarm. Nurses, orderlies and staff came rushing out and the ladies were both taken in on stretchers. A Squadron Leader asked what had happened and he in turn rushed into the hospital. He was a Senior Medical Officer. Yet another approached Freddie, remarking on the state he was in. He was ordered to clean himself up and take the car back to the motor compound and wait there for Flt Robertson.

On his arrival at the compound the Flt wanted a full report. By now Freddie was getting angry, nobody it seemed cared about him or the state he was in. To them the car was more important. As he gathered up his personal belongings he noticed Mrs Churton's handbag on the floor. He quickly retrieved it and put it beside his own personal items. Also, where Mrs Elison had been sitting there were two very shiny round things like small medals. When he picked them up he was surprised how heavy they were. He hid them too. At last the RAF saw fit to look after him and drove him to his billet to get cleaned up. By now it was late afternoon and in his anger, instead of taking the handbag and the two medals to the Orderly Room, he sought out Mr Jones and on reporting to him as instructed gave the handbag to him.

Mr Jones was very excited and he tipped Mrs Churton's handbag out, but he found nothing. Freddie had beaten him to it. Mr Jones looked disappointed, but then Freddie produced the two medals.

"Ah, that's what I want, well done, Airman. How did you find these little beauties? Good chap and well done. Tell me, where did you find these?" Freddie told him.

Mr Jones, stroking his chin was thinking hard.

"No matter what happens tomorrow, report to me first, is that understood?"

"Yes sir," he replied, "but what shall we do about Mrs Churton's handbag?"

"I like the word 'we' Airman. Don't get too carried away."

"No sir, not in that way, I meant shall I take it to the hospital. I would like to know at least how she is."

"By all means and try to give it to her personally, if only for your own sake."

Freddie was a little apprehensive as he approached the hospital and on arriving at the main entrance and going inside he was immediately challenged by a senior N.C.O.

"What do you think you're doing in here Airman? You are out of bounds." Freddie tried to explain but the N.C.O. would have none of it.

However, his last effort to put Freddie down failed because he was making so much noise that he attracted the attention of the Matron of the Queen Mary's Nursing Service. Freddie stood his ground and explained that as it was Mrs Churton's handbag and he had discovered it in the car she was in and, since he was the driver, that he should give it to her personally. The Matron did not seem quite sure what to do and told him to wait about five minutes. Later the Matron appeared with Wing

Commander Churton who overruled everyone and he took Freddie into a small room where Deborah was recovering. She too had heard the commotion and it had woken her up from her sleep. Freddie stood to attention and gave the handbag to her. She in turn gave it to her husband and asked him to empty it out and throw it away. Freddie quietly asked her how she was.

"I am much better now and thanks for all you did." The Matron came in and ordered the Wing Commander and Freddie out.

"Mrs Churton must have rest." The Wing Commander kissed her hand and touching her brow, said, "See you tomorrow," and left. There was nothing mentioned of Mrs Elison whatsoever so he left it at that. There was a film show on that night so he went to see it and it took the day's events off his mind.

CHAPTER 4

The next day Freddie reported to the Wing Commander who told him that he did not require his car that particular day and would he report to Flt Lt Robertson for instructions. When he reported to Flt Lt Robertson he had no driving duties for him but he was asked to report to Mr Jones. On doing just that Mr Jones told him that the two medals were not medals at all but were gold sovereigns. Freddie was still in the dark.

"Do I have to spell it out to you Airman what they are?"

"Yes sir you do."

"Well they were in their day like a pound note before England introduced paper money."

Ah, thought Freddie, that's why his mother got annoyed when his grandma always offered a ten-shilling note as half a sovereign.

"Well sir, I must be honest with you that until yesterday I had never heard of a gold sovereign, let alone seen or held one."

Mr Jones immediately responded with an apology. "Well Airman I had better come clean with you. During operations both in Europe and out here in the Far East agents would buy local loyalty for intelligence with gold sovereigns. It always worked. Gold. Gold, young man is the most desirable metal in the whole world."

Mr Jones looked at his watch and muttered to himself, "Mmm... one and a half hours, it should be enough. Well Airman, I'm going to take a chance with you."

Freddie wondered what was coming next. Mr Jones said to him:

"My name is not Mr Jones but Lt Colonel Hontas of the British Services Special Investigation Branch, SIB, and I have been sent here to investigate a very large robbery. Have you heard anything in the past three months about such a robbery?"

"No sir, I haven't, nothing at all."

"No, that's because it has been kept a secret; only a few people know. Now when I tell you, you will be one more. That is why you were picked to be the Wing Commander's official driver. So when you brought me his wife's handbag and the two gold sovereigns, I was impressed. Now, in the Station Commander's office there is a safe where all valuables and cash are kept and our problem begins because, at the time of the robbery, only two officers knew the combination of the safe, the C.O. and Wing Commander Churton. But both of them have been cleared as both have watertight alibis. So somewhere on this station there is a very good safe cracker. But we are not ruling anyone out. Now when you gave me those two sovereigns it told me that the loot was probably still on the station. But before I tell you any more, I want you to sign this form. It is the Official Secrets Act and I must warn you if so much as divulge any information to anyone other than an S.I.B. Officer, you will be in a lot of trouble. Do you understand?"

Freddie hesitated but spluttered out, "Yes I do sir."

"Now before you sign you have 24 hours to make up your mind. Here are some pluses. In brief, you will be given a special pass and be paid extra money, both here and when you get back to the U.K. And there is more. Now off you go and report to me tomorrow at 09.00 hours to tell me yes or no."

Freddie got out of the chair, stood to attention, saluted and left.

CHAPTER 5

When Freddie got back to his billet he decided to give it much thought. In a way it appealed to him, but he was a little scared at first. Some of his mates even remarked how much quieter he was than usual but he put them off by saying he had received a bad letter from home. They pressed him but he would not elaborate, so they left him alone. As he was about to make his mind up to say 'no', something came into his head which made him think again. Two people came to his mind whom he wanted to protect, the Wing Commander and certainly his wife. This tipped the balance, so 'yes' it was.

Next day he reported to Lt Col. Hontas as ordered. The Lt Col. told him that for a few years he would be a very minor player. Also he would receive special training on how to do things, but for now that would have to wait.

The following day he resumed his normal duties driving the Wing Commander wherever he had to go. On the way back to base the Wing Commander told Freddie to stop and pull over to the side of the road. The Wing Commander got out, came round the car and sat in the front passenger seat. He offered Freddie a cigarette and he lit up as well. Also he took out a hip flask and took a long swig from it.

"Ah that's better, I needed that," he said. "Now look here, we get on all right don't we?"

"Yes sir we do."

"And you get on with my wife, am I right?"
"Yes sir, I think she is a very nice lady."
"Well old chap she certainly likes you."
"Thank you sir."

"Now here's something else. How would you like to have your own room, albeit a small one, in our villa? You could eat and sleep there but you can still do your own thing off duty. Also you can have the same food more or less as we have. Our cook is very good."

"Thank you very much sir, it sounds very agreeable."

"That's that then, you can move in over the next two days. Don't worry, I've cleared it with Flt Robertson. OK then, off we go old chap, tally ho, back to base."

During the rest of the day Freddie started to get all of his kit gathered together and moved into his new billet. He also informed Lt Col. Hontas what had been arranged.

"Good," he exclaimed, "you will be closer to them, but be careful."

On settling in, his first knock on his door was none other than Mrs Churton. She told him it would be the best for everyone and she said she was pleased for him. Also, everyone from the porter upwards had been given instructions how to behave towards him.

"Thank you, Madam, you're most kind."

After Christmas 1946 the first big social event was the New Year's Eve party. It was held at the District Officer's house where anyone who was anyone was invited. 1947 was going to be a year of change. Burma had been given a date for its independence in January 1948, but there was a rumour going around that India would get hers in 1947. A lot of people thought it was too quick, but the Labour Government in London wanted it over and done with. As a result, the very good lifestyle enjoyed by the Raj and all the others, i.e. the Army, the R.A.F. and their wives, was coming to an end, so the unofficial order of the day was 'let's make merry while it lasts'.

Well into the New Year, news was coming in of the plight of dear old England. It seems she was having the coldest, longest winter in nearly eighty years. In fact things and life in general were far worse than in the darkest days of the war, but some personnel and their wives had to go back sooner rather than later. One of these was Flt and Mrs Elison.

Freddie took them to the airfield in the car and Mrs Elison shook hands with him saying goodbye and thanking him for how he had rushed Mrs Churton and herself to the hospital when they had food poisoning.

"It was my duty, Madam. Goodbye and good luck."

CHAPTER 6

In April, when the Wing Commander did not require the car but Mrs Churton did, she gave him instructions where she wished to go, but first she asked if he would drive to the Army married quarters to call on a Mrs Baskey.

On the way Deborah said to Freddie, "What do you do when my husband or myself do not want the car?" He said that, providing Flt Robertson did not want him for any other driving, he attended classes and lectures at the education service.

"Oh, that's a surprise to me. What subjects are you taking?"

"Things in general Madam, but in particular business and economics because when I get demobbed I would like to make things from special orders as I am now a fully-qualified carpenter joiner."

"Well we must keep in touch when we all get back home."

"Yes Madam."

As she left the car she said, "I'll try not to be too long. Mrs Baskey and I are arranging a big party. I will make sure you get something to eat and drink."

"Thank you."

She had been gone about two hours. It did bother Freddie as he was used to waiting. However, she suddenly appeared alone, walking or stumbling across the drive. As he looked up he saw her fall over. He rushed to her and lifted her up and got her to the car.

He thought, my God, she's had plenty, she's drunk. He settled her in and asked her did she wish to go now or wait.

"No wait, wait," she said. "I must talk to you, you alone. I know I am the worse for drink as you can see, but the reason I'm like this is because I want Dutch courage."

Freddie was getting a bit on edge and uncomfortable. She broke her silence with a slightly stunning question.

"Freddie darling, about half way back to base could you stop the car and make out something is wrong? I must talk to you."

Freddie chose a spot to pull over, lifted the bonnet and unscrewed the radiator tap to let out some water. She asked him what he was doing. He said, "If anyone wants to know, such as the Military Police, the car was overheating and was losing water."

"Very clever, darling. You are very clever."

"Now you must stop calling me Freddie and darling. It is not right. If you are not careful you and I will be in trouble."

"Oh well, if that's your attitude, forget it. I have misjudged you." She got out of the car and stood with her back to him. He broke the situation by saying sorry and he said it made him frightened.

"Don't be," she retorted, "I can get you out of any trouble you like to name. Now come on, join me with a cigarette." She gave him one of hers and cupped her hands round his, giving him the most sensual look he had ever been given. Now she asked him if everything about the car was ready.

"Yes I think it looks like a genuine breakdown."

"Now listen Freddie to what I have to say. A few days ago I had a letter from Joan Elison saying what happened to everyone who was returning home from abroad, particularly officers and their wives. With hardly any exceptions their luggage and personal belongings were searched, in fact they knew the stations, bases and airfields where everyone came from. Mrs Elison and some other wives from RAF Maggadore were semi strip-searched. She found out they were looking for valuable jewellery and some gold coins, but found nothing. So she advised me to be careful and also to buy some cheap bazaar jewellery to declare and put them off. These people are Customs and Excise. Joan was very frightened and upset. Here, here, Freddie, you read it yourself."

Inwardly he was not surprised, knowing what he did about the safe robbery. Deborah took it back from him and set it alight. Just then a Jeep pulled up, it was the military police (red caps): one officer, one sergeant, a corporal and a driver. Naturally the officer spoke first to Deborah, who was casually supported by the car as she could not stand up without support. The Lt Wild enquired what the trouble was.

"Ask my husband's personal driver, he will tell you."

The Lt went over to Freddie and asked him. "She's over-heated that's all sir. I've drained the radiator to let her cool down." The Lt started to fuss over Deborah, but she gave him short shrift; and the military police went on their way.

"Joan Elison told me that you have to pay duty on them. I have also heard from a good source that lower ranks very seldom or never get stopped, the reason being there are too many of you to deal with. Also, your pay is so little that you can't buy anything of value, so that is another reason they don't bother, which brings me to ask, would you bring my valuables back with you. I promise here and now I will make it worth your while. How about it? I don't want an answer now but do think it over. At the moment we have plenty of time. The latest I have heard from my husband is July. You can now see, Freddie dear, why I have had... hic... a lot to drink. They call it Dutch courage."

Freddie was taken aback. He suggested that he should get the car going and make for base. When he had started the car and lowered the bonnet, Deborah was sitting in the front. This in turn made him annoyed. She was going too far. He pleaded with her to go to the rear seat but she would have none of it. Now as tipsy as she was she knew what she had done. She was going to do as he said but in temper he started up the car and drove off as fast as the car would go. About three miles from base she threw her handbag onto the rear seat. She asked him to slow down and she climbed over to get to where she should be. He looked at what she was doing. All at once she was all tits, bums and legs. When she landed on the rear floor she burst out laughing and so did he, especially when she tucked in one of her breasts which had fallen out.

While all of this was going on he had stopped the car. So far they had got away with it. Laughter does not last very long. He gave her some time to adjust herself and when she got out of the car back at base nothing was said by either. Freddie took the car back to the motor compound and to play safe reported that it had a water leak. He walked back to the main base to cool off. Usually he would get a lift. While walking he said to himself, 'that's it, it has gone too far. Everything is on her terms; she has what the S.I.B. is looking for.' He was now approaching Lt Col. Hontas' office to tell him about what had happened and ask him to get him back onto normal driving duties. He then began to feel better.

CHAPTER 7

Arriving at the Lt Colonel's office, he found it to be closed, all locked up. Now what should he do? He became confused and it suddenly dawned on him he had to go back to the Wing Commander's villa because he was billeted there. He had no choice. But to return to where she was living, where he was living... He got to his quarters and the cook gave him his meal. Afterwards it was cigarette after cigarette until it made him ill. He couldn't read or do anything. In desperation he asked the housekeeper's husband, who acted as his butler, to get him a large whisky from the Wing Commander's cabinet. He sipped it and then went to bed, hoping when he awoke it had all been a dream.

Now something else woke him. He could hear raised voices. It was the Wing Commander and Madam, but he could not quite hear what it was about. But he did pick up something like, "Take the bloody lot for all I care." And then it went quiet, so he drifted off to sleep once more. It was 11.30. At about 2 am there was a knock on his door, not loud but enough to wake him again.

"Freddie... Freddie..." in a low-pitched voice. "Please let me in. Please."

He could do no more but let her in, if only to find out what had been happening. As he opened the door she fell into his arms crying.

"Madam, do you realise where you are and what you are doing?"

"Freddie, I no longer care, please hold me, I beg of you."

His first reply was, "What would happen if your husband found you here?" She told him he was out for the count. He had been drinking and had taken sleeping tablets as well. It took her a long time to stop crying. When things calmed down they both sat on the edge of his bed. It was he who offered her a cigarette. Again she cupped her hands around his as they lit up.

"Now what is this all about?" She told him she was sorry about what she had asked him to do for her and sorry again about the remark about lower ranks not being searched on arriving back in England.

"That was really nasty of me, please forgive me, would you?"

"Yes of course I will. Now go back to bed and take one of your husband's tablets and get a good night's sleep or what's left of it. Don't worry, we are friends again." He thought… anything to get rid of her.

Freddie was again disturbed at 6.45 am by Devendra the housekeeper and cook shouting, "Sab... Sab... Come quickly!"

Half awake, he opened his door and asked what the matter was.

"Much trouble, Sab, please come." Getting dressed as quickly as he could he followed her into the Wing Commander's bedroom. She indicated in her own way that she could not wake the Wing Commander or his wife. They were still warm but appeared unconscious. He immediately 'phoned the Adjutant and he, in turn, got in touch with the Senior Medical Officer. While he waited he hid the half-empty whisky bottle, took the glasses and quickly washed them and took one glass back with water. He left the bottle of sleeping tablets where it was. He then went round to Deborah's side and held her hand, gently stroking it.

He heard the front door open and quickly let go. In they came, the Adjutant and the M.O. The M.O. examined the Wing Commander first and somehow brought him round, all be it in a daze. Deborah came around without any help. Freddie stood to attention. In what seemed a short time they were both sitting up in bed wondering what all the fuss was about. The M.O. ordered everyone out of the room.

Freddie got himself washed and shaved ready to see the Adjutant as he had requested. He marched into his office and was told to stand at ease. "Now Airman, this is just a preliminary talk off the record. Now up to the moment when you were alerted by the servants, did you hear or see anything unusual?"

"No sir, nothing at all after supper. I stayed in my room and read my book, although I did feel a bit queasy and I kept yawning. But I was not tired in myself, but I fell asleep while reading. I thought it best to turn in."

"Well that will be all for now. We must wait and see what the M.O. has decided to do. All right, go back to your quarters until further notice, you are dismissed."

CHAPTER 8

At times in life everyone needs a little bit of luck and Freddie got his. When he got back to the villa Deborah was alone. He asked her did Madam require any transport, giving her a wink as he did so. She took the hint.

"Well yes, I think a drive to the Wives' Club will do me good after what has happened."

"Very good Madam. I'll report back here in about an hour." He cleared it with the Adjutant and requested a car from Flt Robertson. In fact it was the one that had the fake leak. When they arrived at the Wives' Club they were the first to arrive. The grounds were empty and it gave them a chance to have a serious talk. Deborah began by saying that she had been semi-conscious when he had taken the whisky away and cleaned the glasses and asked him why he had done that. Freddie said that had the whisky and the sleeping tablets been side by side, the M.O. would have put two and two together and her husband would most probably have been in trouble. She had noticed in the tone of his voice he was angry at something and she asked him what the matter was. He told her he was sick to death with everything. It had got to the stage where, for a start, he did not know how to address her.

He asked her a question, "Do I call you... Madam... Mrs Churton, Deborah or what?"

She snapped back at him, "Oh, it's the rank again is it?"

"Yes it is rank, all the bloody time it's rank, rank, and it's getting me down. I want to get home and get demobbed and be myself. Do you understand, Madam?"

She got out of the rear seat and came into the front and sat beside him. "Now look, if anything you and I are the same in many ways. I too am fed up with the RAF and all that goes on. All of it is a charade, a bloody farce, but we have to stick it out. Please Freddie, don't let us fall out. Let us be friends, true friends."

By now they were holding hands. "Yes, all right, but tell me why were you and your husband having that row. All I picked up was 'take the bloody lot'. I assume it was the sleeping tablets, that is why I cleaned up before the MO arrived."

"Believe me sweetheart, I cannot tell you now but one day when you are Mr F W Radnor Esquire, I will tell you and I will reward you when I do. Are we friends again?" Pleading with him.

His reply was, "I don't think we ever really fell out."

As a car appeared she quickly kissed his hand, disappeared from the front seat, blew him a kiss and resumed the charade of social niceness at the club.

She left the club and sat down where she should officially be, in the back seat. "Now listen Freddie, I have given what we talked about some thought. When we are alone I want you to call me Deborah and I will call you Freddie, but at all other times it must be Mrs Churton. How about that, but I don't really mean it. Does that sound all right to you?"

"Yes it does, at least it clears the air." When they got back to base she ran into the villa and Freddie walked to his rooms. As he was freshening up there was a knock on the door. By now he recognised who it was. As he opened the door, he saw that he was right. Deborah made no attempt to come in but just said, "My husband is all right but he must take it easy for a week or so."

"That is good news Mrs Churton. Will I be getting any special duties or so on?"

"My husband has indicated that he would like you to stay and do things on a day-to-day basis."

"Yes, I understand." With that she shook his hand and gave him a wink which he returned.

The next day he was able to see the Lt Colonel. Freddie told him what had happened – only his version. As for anything else, he had nothing to report. The Lt Colonel told him that apart from speculation and the two gold sovereigns, he had got nowhere, so the powers that be had decided to close the case, unless something turned up by itself. To finish, the Lt Colonel put his hand in his pocket and gave Freddie a gold sovereign. "Here, take it. You haven't done much, but we know you. Keep it safe, it will always be something for you to fall back on. Sew it into the lining of your regular uniform. When you get demobbed you will be contacted at some time. The code word or letter will be *'Indian Lily'*. You understand, don't you?"

"Yes sir." Freddie saluted and said goodbye.

CHAPTER 9

It was now mid-May and the monsoon season began. At its height the rain and storms bring with them much boredom to the station and the airfield is brought to a standstill. On one particular evening when it was really bad, Freddie was alternating between listening to the radio and reading. At about 8 o'clock Deborah gave her usual knock. He let her in, leaving the door open. She said that her husband and herself were bored stiff and asked him if he would like to join them for a drink.

"Thank you Madam but that is against the rules."

She agreed but said, "I don't think anyone is about to go snooping around tonight." He readily accepted, provided the Wing Commander approved.

"Of course he has. Don't worry."

As he got to their lounge, he was encouraged by the Wing Commander to relax. "It's OK," he said. "Come and sit down."

Freddie enquired, "Sir, do you play cards?"

"Well yes, we sometimes play bridge."

"Only I was thinking it's just the evening for a game and there are three of us." Deborah shouted with elation at Freddie's suggestion and over the first drink decided what game to play. At about 11.30 the Wing Commander said, "Make this the last hand and we'll finish." When the time came, Deborah said to her husband:

"Darling, this has been one of the best evenings we have had for a long time," and he agreed, thanking Freddie for thinking of it.

"Goodnight sir and goodnight Madam."

He could not give her a wink as sir was looking straight at him.

The next morning there was a loud knock on Freddie's door. It was the Wing Commander saying, "Quick Aircraftsman, get your cape, I must get to the runway. There's an Air France DC3, it has had a bumpy landing and is stranded at the end of the runway." There were vehicles of all sorts there and the passengers were being helped out of the aircraft. They were a mixture of military and civil servants going home on leave from French Indo China. Everyone was taken to the terminal building where the CO had just arrived. The aircraft was not too badly damaged but the occupants were a bit shaken. Most of them were officers and high-ranking civilians. It was agreed that they would be billeted out among the station's married quarters. The Wing Commander volunteered to take in the crew as he had room to spare. The Wing Commander asked Freddie how many the car could take.

"At a pinch, sir, six."

"Good, that is the entire crew. You take them to the villa and ask Mrs Churton to make them feel at home, then come back for me and their luggage." Deborah would be in her element. She liked things with a purpose. As they got into the car, sitting next to Freddie was a very petite and attractive cabin stewardess and she sat so close to him he could feel her warm body next to him. As she got in she said, "Bonjour Monsieur." He did not know what it meant but replied, "Hello."

At the villa Deborah greeted them and then Freddie returned to the terminal building. Again the car was well loaded, this time with the luggage. Deborah met them at the main door. "That will be all for now, Airman, thank you, but stay in your room until further orders." Sometime later, Deborah came and said, "I must go to the service stores to get more food. The cabin steward is coming with us as she will be able to advise me what to get." Both got in the front seat, with Deborah sitting next to Freddie. 'My, my,' he thought, 'she is really enjoying this.'

They came out with boxes of food, all of which were then put on the back seats. Freddie went to get in; the cabin steward had beaten Deborah to the centre position. Deborah was put out and she showed it, but said nothing. When they got back to the villa, everyone went their own ways. About an hour later, the Wing Commander knocked on Freddie's door. He asked him if he would be prepared to give up the room where he sat and had his meals. Freddie was taken aback as the Wing Commander did not order him to do so, nor call his name. The Wing Commander said he was very reluctant to order him to do so.

Freddie said, "Yes sir, that's all right, I'll collect my things now." A single bed was brought in with some luggage and then the person who was to sleep there entered the room – it was none other than the very pretty cabin stewardess. Freddie helped make up the bed and was introduced to her – her name was Denise. She said, "Merci."

When it was time for the evening meal a new problem appeared – where to eat it? Without too much fuss they improvised as best they could. Later on Freddie invited his unexpected but welcome guest to the station cinema where the latest film release was showing. As they entered the cinema, there was a lot of wolf whistling from some of his unit. Freddie was not annoyed but in a way rather pleased with himself. Getting back to the villa Denise thanked him, gave him the slightest of cheek kisses and said "Bonsoir."

About two hours later, there was a gentle knock on the door separating his bedroom and hers. He was still reading. The door opened and Denise came in, apologising and saying she could not sleep, indicating the bed was too small and uncomfortable. He said to her, "Let us change over," as before he had become the Wing Commander's driver he had slept on a bed like that.

"You are so kind Monsieur Freddie." For a while they sat on the edge of his bed talking. She then suddenly got up, went back to her room and came back with a bottle of something. As it opened the cork popped much too loudly, so much so that footsteps could be heard outside. However, lights were soon put out and all was quiet. He asked what was in the bottle and she said it was champagne. Quietly Freddie fetched two glasses and so for Freddie at least he was going to achieve two firsts that night – his first glass of champagne and his first taste of the delights of the act of love. To him the first taste was disappointing but out of politeness he said it was nice. Denise said it was not up to much as it had not been served chilled. Also the glasses were not right. However, she downed hers then made her move. She did literally hand herself to him on a plate. Neither bothered to undress. She had in her hand a French letter and proceeded to put it on Freddie. What she felt was enormous but she herself was very excited and she only got it on halfway when he ejaculated. It was all over the place. When he returned from paradise he said to her how sorry he felt but he said it was his first time. She reassured him and told him to wait and it would soon come back. She poured them both another glass of champagne.

"This drink will relax you," she said as she started to dry him and at the same time undress him. Also, she put out the light, again reassuring him to relax. "Here you put it on yourself, it will be better." And it was. He entered her and got into a rhythm. It was wonderful. She whispered, "When I bite you, try and let it go and we'll rise together." For her he was a dream, to him she was the most beautiful girl in all the world.

CHAPTER 10

In the morning Denise was called away, along with all the crew and passengers, to a meeting to tell them that, all being well and subject to getting the all clear from the senior ground engineer, they would be leaving in about forty-eight hours, and that until further notice everyone could do as they wished. Most wanted to see the local town and do some shopping. The CO gave the Wing Commander permission to arrange everything. Deborah got in on the action and with her husband arranged the trip. Other vehicles were drafted in and the crew opted for Freddie's car. Again Denise sat next to him in the front. They arrived near the town centre and all the vehicles were parked near the police station. Denise said to Freddie:

"Are you coming with us?"

"No," said Freddie, "we must all stay with our vehicles."

When they all came back some had really gone to town so much that the Flight Captain said, "We must be careful we don't take off overweight."

Back at the villa after dinner, Denise and Freddie sat talking about each other's lives. Freddie insisted Denise spoke first. She began by saying that her parents worked a small farm in central France, adding that her father was a very good farmer and every few years acquired more land. During the war it had been terrible. Everyone was frightened of the Germans – one never knew what those bastards would do next.

"I was my Pappa's girl. I was the only girl and I had two brothers to protect me. My father made within the house a secret hiding place for me in case of a round-up. It was stocked with some food and water so I might be saved. One of my brothers was a POW and the other stayed on the farm until it was too dangerous, so he left and joined the Resistance up in the mountains. One day in late 1943 my father was in one of his fields when he came across an injured RAF man. He had a wound and a broken leg. My Pappa was always reluctant to get involved but he felt so sorry for him that after dark he got him into the house and hid him where I was to hide. He then called the local doctor to attend him. Now, Mon Ami, it seems the RAF have come to my rescue. In the evenings I used to sit by our RAF guest to keep him company and that is how I learned to speak English. Like you, Mon Ami, he was, how you say, a shy English gentleman. Also, that is how I became a cabin steward. I beat a lot of other girls for the job because of one of your countrymen teaching me.

He felt much at ease in her company, so easy that he could ask her anything. After what happened on that unforgettable night he plucked up courage to ask her if she was she able to take things home to France and did she ever go on flights to London. "Yes I do, in fact if the rota has not changed it will be my next call."

He said to her, "Denise, please forgive me for asking but could you take a small parcel to England and post it to an address there for Mrs Churton. As far as I can tell you will not be in any trouble and it will help me as well as her."

She hesitated but said, "I will try, especially for you." Freddie asked to see Mrs Churton or the Wing Commander about any duties for the following day. Deborah came down from upstairs and played the ruse.

He also said the French cabin steward wanted to see her – it's a woman's thing. Freddie briefed her on what he had suggested and she thought it was a good idea. He ushered her into Denise's room and after a few moments Freddie was called in. It was a three-way arrangement. Deborah thanked Denise and said, "You will be well rewarded." Denise said it was for Freddie and no-one else. They agreed the package must be as small as possible so she could conceal it on her body. Deborah was excited and left, giving him a wink as she went.

Later that evening Denise knocked on Freddie's door. She had another bottle of champagne – the cork going pop once more. She told him not to worry about the parcel: "We do it all the time. Nearly everyone at each end does it." Denise then came out with something which took Freddie by surprise and alarmed him. It was, "Madame Churton, she seems to be in love with you, Mon Ami."

"How do you know?"

"Ah, I have watched her, particularly when you are near to her. Do you love her?" she enquired.

He replied, "I don't know, but I would do anything for her and I would protect her as much as I would protect you in any way I could." For this last remark Denise gave him an embrace and a kiss, not a passionate one but as a friend.

Next day news came through that the DC3 had been passed for service. Last-minute packing was hurriedly put together. Denise said she was sorry about the state of the room but Freddie told her not to worry because the servants would see to it. When they got to the car, Deborah was already sitting in the front seat. This time it was Denise's turn to be put out. During the ride to the airfield Deborah's hand went behind Freddie's back and she seductively kept moving it about. Also, the parcel was passed to Denise. Freddie hoped that both had taken his advice not to put the address it was to be sent to until it could be posted in England. By doing that no names would be discovered.

Denise said, "Goodbye, mon amour, see you some time." As she was the steward it was her duty to stand at the door to check and welcome her passengers. All was correct and with a final wave to him – he was sure her wave was to him only – she closed the door, the undercarriage wheel chocks were taken away and the aircraft taxied to the end of the runway. Air France flight number SR127 had permission to take off into the blue sky of India.

"Well there they go," said the Wing Commander. He told Freddie to drop him off at station HQ and to take Mrs Churton back to the villa where she had to supervise the cleaning up after their guests. The villa had been locked up while they were at the airfield and Deborah opened the main door. Freddie was expecting instructions to muster all the servants but she said nothing. In they both went and somehow by instinct made their way to his quarters. She led the way and went straight into the room where Denise had slept.

She came running out, heading straight for him. "Hold me, Freddie, hold me please." He had no choice. She buried her head between his neck and his shoulder. After what seemed minutes, he felt her loosen her grip and asked her what was the matter.

"I don't want you to go into her room."

"Why ever not? I must," he insisted to her and there on the unmade bed was a parcel, a letter and a bottle of whisky. On the envelope it read 'To Freddie, avec amour.' The paper was heavily perfumed. This was the reason Deborah had come running out to him; she had immediately seen Denise as her rival. He turned round and there she stood. She was at that moment in time the most helpless, vulnerable woman in the world. She knew it and so did he. He embraced her again and whispered through her long blonde hair, "It's all right. It's you I love, it's you I love."

It was what she wanted to hear and so they broke away. "Let's have a cigarette – there's no substitute at times like this. Well let's see what's in your parcel. Shall I open it for you?"

"If you want to, go on then." When the parcel was undone, Denise had bought him a red dressing gown. He remarked:

"Goodness, what a wonderful present!"

Deborah could do no more but agree, saying:

"What a terrific colour, the colour of love!"

Her doubts soon came back but she hid her inner feelings from him. At this point whatever might have happened was interrupted by noises and so their moments alone ended. Deborah went off to get her home back into shape and Freddie did the same. He was missing Denise already.

His next problem was the bottle of whisky – what to do with it? So, when he called at HQ to pick up the Wing Commander, he asked for his advice. Both the Wing Commander and Freddie were sure it was against regulations so he offered it to the Wing Commander. This touched him deeply, especially since at the same time he had to agree that it was the best solution. Before he got out of the car, Freddie asked him if he knew of anyone he could trust who would translate his letter from Denise from French into English. The Wing Commander said he would put out a few feelers.

CHAPTER 11

A further week passed but nothing happened. It was now the last week of June and news came through that India would get its independence at midnight on the 14th of August 1947. Things were happening very fast now. The next day Deborah said to Freddie that she had found a lady who would translate his letter. She was the French-born wife of a civil servant and would be at the final grand ball to be held on the 2nd of July, and Deborah would introduce her to him.

The day before the grand ball Freddie was told by the Wing Commander that, in about two weeks' time he and Mrs Churton would be leaving India and returning home to England.

Freddie said, "Will you be glad sir?"

"Yes," came the reply, "very much so. It's been over three years since my wife last saw her parents and that goes for me as well." Then he asked Freddie how much longer he had still to serve.

"Next year some time, sir."

On the morning of the great farewell ball, as it had now become known, Deborah came to Freddie's quarters. This time she was so excited that she didn't bother to knock. She caught him in his dressing gown, a garment unheard of, let alone possessed, by the working class. It dampened her excitement as it was connected to Denise.

All the same she said, "Freddie, my mother received the parcel. Your room friend posted it in England. How did you think of that, it was a good idea?"

Freddie just shrugged his shoulders and said, "Good" and left it at that.

Deborah remarked, "It's a big day today."

Freddie said, "Yes Madam, they are calling it the end of an era." She was perturbed by the coldness of his reply. She returned to him in the same manner, telling him where he would be given orders for the day and arrangements for the evening.

When the time came to leave for the ball, the Wing Commander told him to go to the CO's villa to collect the CO's wife. Freddie had never seen her close up. She never even acknowledged him. The venue was about twenty miles away. Freddie drew up at the main entrance then parked the car in the space that had been allocated. After about half an hour he looked up and coming towards him was Deborah and a lady who it turned out was the person who was going to translate Denise's letter. Deborah introduced him to Mrs Greerson and at the same time handed him a large whisky and soda giving him a wink which he returned. The incident earlier in the day seemed to have evaporated.

Simone Greerson looked quickly at the letter and said, "It is too dark out here, do you mind young man if I take it into my quarters? Would you like me to put the translation on a separate piece of paper?" Freddie agreed and said he would like that.

"Very well, but it will take me a while as I have guests to see to." Deborah chipped in saying that Freddie had got until the end of the night. The remark did not go down well with Mrs Greerson or with Freddie. He returned to the car, lit a cigarette and enjoyed his whisky.

Suddenly he heard footsteps coming nearer. It was someone in a huge hurry and in fact it was Mrs Greerson. She asked Freddie what he had been up to. At this he was dumbfounded, saying:

"Nothing Madam. What is the matter?"

"Well the matter is what this young lady friend of yours has put in her letter to you. Before I put it on paper I had better read it out to you, but not here. I will speak to Mrs Churton and arrange something. Here is your letter, keep it safe and Mrs Churton will tell you where or when. It will probably be at her villa. I will have to find some excuse to go there. Now I must go. Bonsoir Monsieur."

Deborah was as anxious to know what was in the letter as Freddie was, so she quickly thought up a ruse to get Mrs Greerson over to the villa in next to no time. She made sure Freddie would be there and Mrs Greerson drew up in her husband's official car. For a moment or two he was more interested in the car than anything else. The driver was Indian. Deborah called him in and all three sat at a small table in an ante room.

Mrs Greerson asked him if he minded Mrs Churton being in the room or would he like her to leave. Freddie said he would like her to leave.

"Very well then." On the nod from Mrs Greerson, Deborah got up and left, then Mrs Greerson suggested they should walk in the garden. The letter read:

'Mon Freddie,

'May I thank you for making my enforced stay in your quarters a very pleasant one. I hope you do not think ill of me for forcing myself upon you on that unforgettable night. I did it for two reasons. The first reason happened a week before our plane which so nearly crashed at your airfield, left Saigon. You see I had a note left at my flat in Paris from my fiancé breaking off

our engagement. I was so upset that I did some stupid things.

'I stole some money, two bottles of champagne, a bottle of whisky and other things. I was in a rage. The second was when your lovely RAF came to our rescue. It was then that I first saw you. You are a very handsome and good-looking young man. I fell for you there and then. Because of God's monsoon and landing at your airfield, fate took a hand for us to meet. But most of all your handsome Wing Commander putting me in the room next to you. That night my emotions took over and above all else, Mon Ami, you helped me forget.

'Hopefully we shall meet again. You can write to my flat in Paris or my home. It is said one never forgets the first person you make love to. I hope you never forget me, mon amour. Denise 'mot'

Mrs Greerson broke the silence by saying, "Take my advice young man and try to remember, but destroy the letter."

Simone Greerson then asked him, "Did Denise give you anything more than her body?"

"Yes," Freddie replied, "a red dressing gown."

"Is that all? Are you sure?"

"Yes," he confirmed. Then the three of them went to his quarters and he unwrapped it and showed her.

"My God," Simone said, "it is beautiful and a very expensive one. You know if you are caught with this they are going to ask questions. It's a pity to destroy it. Has anyone got any ideas?" Deborah of all people suggested that perhaps Simone could get it to England for him and then post it to his home. It was a good idea and Mrs Greerson agreed. "I'll do it for you Airman, and Denise. My husband and myself have diplomatic immunity."

Freddie went to his quarters to make up the parcel. He had plenty of packaging but no string and he had to ask Deborah for some. All done he gave it to Mrs Greerson and thanked her many times over.

CHAPTER 12

Three days later when Freddie reported for the day's orders, the Wing Commander had some good news for him. It was that orders had come through for him to return to a new posting in the UK and so of course Mrs Churton would be accompanying him as well. Inwardly Freddie was relieved. He wanted to return to normal driving duties.

The day of their departure arrived. Much of their luggage had to go in another aircraft. As they left the villa they turned round to have a last look at the home they had shared for four years. What luggage they would take with them was put on the back seat, so Wing Commander and Mrs Churton sat in the front, she of course in the middle next to her driver. Again her arm slid between his back and the seat.

On arrival the aircraft was waiting. It was a DC3 that had come up from Rangoon. Porters took their luggage and Deborah said goodbye first and gave him a wink. She would have liked to have given him a kiss but of course she could not do so. She stepped aside for the Wing Commander and they saluted each other. For the first time he called him Fred.

"It's Freddie," Deborah said angrily. Not for the first time her husband ignored her. They were the last to board the plane and she wanted to turn and wave, but could not. It was chocks away and Flight 237 taxied to the end of the runway. As the wind was coming from the southeast, the plane had to take off into it. She climbed steadily, flying upwards and then banked to the left and so flew back over the airfield. Deborah was sitting next to a port window. Pleasantly surprised, she looked out and she could just make out her Freddie standing next to the car and waving to her. She suddenly burst out crying uncontrollably. Her husband and several of the passengers asked her why and she said, "Just leave me alone, please. Just leave me alone."

Life got back to normal, almost. About a week after he had waved to her, Freddie got instructions to go to the civil servant's home and drive Mrs Simone Greerson to the airfield as she was returning home to England ahead of her husband. When he arrived to call for her, Deborah came back into his mind. He imagined he could smell her perfume.

But, with the appearance of Simone Greerson, the feeling soon went away. Every inch of her was French. Without asking she sat in the front next to him, although there was a distance between them. What was it, he thought to himself, about sitting in the front next to the driver? On the way to the airfield she told him she was taking the same route as Deborah. He was pleased because the Wing Commander had never told him. It appeared they took the DC3 to Bombay and changed to a BOAC Avro York. These aircraft were more comfortable. With a few miles to go, Mrs Greerson told him that had Denise not been French she would have reported her. Freddie was staggered at first but relief soon took over. As she left the car they shook hands and she said something in French which he did not understand. Her plane took off but this time into the wind coming from the west.

A week before India became independent, Freddie was posted to RAF Station Mingladon, Rangoon, in Burma. In turn in 1948 that country too would leave the British Empire and Freddie soon found himself on a ship bound for Singapore, in transit for sailing home and demob. These past seven months had dragged. Deborah had written to him on odd weeks. In one letter she said that apparently when they arrived in England and after a month's leave, the Wing Commander had been selected to attend the RAF Staff College at Bracknell and was given a house in Maidenhead. It appeared he had decided to make the RAF his career. This was good news for Freddie as his home was not far away.

His ship docked at Southampton and on getting ashore he, and a few others were picked out and had their kit searched. He thought, thank God he had nothing with him, meaning Deborah's jewellery. While re-packing he suddenly looked up and caught sight of Lt Colonel Hontas. So that's it. No wonder he was picked out. They thought right, but Denise and Simone Greerson had come to his rescue. After completing all the documentation they were taken to the station. Freddie boarded the train to London, sat down and gave a sigh of relief. He was nearly there, a free man, free of orders, regulations, and above all from the ranking system. He knew it had to be that way but it was not for him. He had seven weeks before he could start work. Getting to Euston he then crossed to Paddington Station.

On the way home the train sped through Maidenhead. Deborah was out there somewhere. Soon he would see her, not as an Airman but as Mr Frederick William Radnor.

CHAPTER 13

Arriving home in May 1946 his family, above all his younger sister Mary, to whom he had addressed the parcel, made a great fuss of him. After things had quietened down he went for a walk to take it all in, but above all to 'phone Deborah. When she lifted the receiver her voice was rapturous with joy. She called him her lovely Freddie.

"My darling, when can we meet?" As his time was his own he suggested she name the place and the day, but in the meantime he told her he would 'phone every day as near to a certain time of day to make sure she was in and alone. Also he suggested that should she not be alone she should say, "You have the wrong number."

On his third call to her she arranged the time of the train he could catch from his local station so that she would be on the platform at Maidenhead. She arrived early and kept looking down the line for the first signs of the train. Then here it came. As it came to a halt several doors opened but she could not catch sight of him. What she was looking for was a man in RAF uniform, but there was no RAF uniform to be seen. Then she noticed a man waving his hand – it was him. She rushed forward, straight into his arms. There they both were, in view of everyone, caution was thrown to the wind. She stood back, holding both his hands, saying, "Oh Freddie, you look wonderful."

They left the station arm-in-arm and Deborah suggested how they would spend the day. However, as the day came to an end some doubts began to trouble him, such as where was all this leading to? She walked to the station with him, still holding hands. She thanked him for a lovely day and said, "We must do this again." She kissed him on the cheek and left him waiting for his train. The porter informed all the intending passengers that the train would be about ten minutes late and this gave Freddie time to reflect on his first meeting with her out of uniform. But reflection did not last but a few moments because he had a tap on the shoulder. He knew who it was before he turned around as he could smell her perfume – it was no cheap shilling-a-bottle stuff, it was hers and hers alone.

As he turned, of course, it was her. She took hold of him and said, "I could not go home knowing you were still in Maidenhead. I will stay and see you on the train and wave to you until you are out of sight." He embraced her and whispered in her ear:

"Oh I do love you so much Deborah." With that his train pulled onto the platform and he got in the carriage, which he had all to himself. He wound down the window, leant out to kiss her, then the train slowly moved along the platform. She blew him a kiss and he returned the gesture, Deborah waving all the time. But just before she was out of sight he noticed she had put a handkerchief to her eyes. This upset him and he was glad at least he had the compartment to himself. He broke his heart crying too, but between stations he composed himself by remembering how many young lovers between 1939 and 1945 had gone through that ritual, some never coming back. Ah, he thought to himself, I'm not going off to war, I will see her again, perhaps in a few days' time. Before he realised it, his destination was near and he left the train a very happy young man.

When he arrived home his mother sensed in her youngest son that something was not quite right. She asked him what was bothering him but he brushed it aside. In haste he replied that it was adjusting to civilian life and his mother accepted his explanation.

After the family had eaten, his siblings did their own thing – Tom went to meet his girlfriend and his elder sister to meet her boyfriend. He envied them because in their relationships the only problem was money, saving and scraping to get married. It was interesting to Freddie how they could do this and that, save here, don't buy this or that. He then perked up after again thinking to himself as he did on the train, at least for the present that problem need not worry me.

From that first meeting they both realised that they were deeply in love, although strangely it was never spoken. No words were about to break free. The affair went on from day to day. There were no restrictions of course when they could meet and be together. The Wing Commander was attending the RAF Staff College at nearby Bracknell from Monday to Friday and came home every day around late afternoon, which was why they had to part so that she was home to greet Maurice. This situation did not bother Freddie as they could see each other every day and for about five to six weeks they more or less did. But the time was fast approaching when his demob. leave would be over and he would have to return to work. In fact that too was fast approaching. The date was the 17th of August. When that date fell, both of them were in for a shock. It would be almost an impossibility to carry on as they had been.

The Monday after the 17th at 8 o'clock he was back in the small factory where he was serving his apprenticeship, which still had two years to run. And there was another problem – apprentices don't earn much money.

Freddie had got through a lot of money, what with train and bus fares, let alone paying for everything he spent on her. He could not see her on weekends so he was able to earn some extra cash by doing odd part-time work most Saturdays. The winter of 1946-7 was very harsh and travel became a nightmare. Except for her letters and his three penny-worth of 'phone calls, in mid-morning lunch break that was all. When the bad winter was coming to an end, all along the Thames Valley was flooded and in one of her letters she told him their house near the river, which was just off Rivermead Road, was under water and they had had to leave. She wrote 'In future, darling, I will be staying with my parents at the address above. Just write once a week, it will have to do for now'. Also she mentioned, as if by a side remark, that she hoped her father would be in a better frame of mind, as the last time she visited them her father stormed off to the pub and had to be rescued by Maurice and brought home dead drunk. It appeared he did not approve of his daughter getting married in India, the reason being he had wanted and dreamed of taking his pure, lovely daughter on his own down the aisle to give her to the man she loved.

The next letter from Deborah was far less romantic than all the previous ones. It was cold and factual and hinted to him that the floods might be a good thing – it was a chance to put an end to the affair. In his way he too was thinking along those lines but the second letter returned to the theme of light-heartedness. It seemed it had the same effect on him and his gloom lifted. Now he was in a place, in a vacuum, where nothing happened. Nowhere.

CHAPTER 14

Midsummer Day was approaching and he was getting plenty of spare work as a result of the bad winter and its consequences. Deborah's letters became less frequent, though the content and tone were different. On arriving home from work one day his mother said to him, "Here son is a telegram. I hope it's not a bad one. Telegrams invariably bring bad news." He took the telegram unopened out into the garden. He was nervous. Somehow he had a feeling it was from her and of course it was. It read: 'Freddie, I must see you. Letter following. Your own Deborah.'

The next morning he left it as late as he could to try to intercept the postman. He could not afford to be late as his boss had recently called him in to the office about the days he had been absent, so he had to wait until dinner time to rush home. In the meantime that morning he had botched a piece of work because he could not concentrate on what he was doing. He felt like a detective taken off a case. The episode upset him. For all intents and purposes he did not return to work for the rest of the day. Had he been a schoolboy it was the equivalent of playing truant. He wrote Deborah a brief letter saying that he could only see her the next day, which was Saturday. He would be off work and said in his letter that he would be waiting outside the saloon bar of the Brown Bear at around midday. He went to the main post office hoping she would receive it the next day. In the letter he assured her in his most affectionate way that if she did not arrive he would not take it as a snub or anything like that. He would understand.

Instead of going by train he went by bus, which would terminate at Maidenhead bus station, a short walk from the rendezvous. Freddie arrived at the Brown Bear quite early and on entering the bar was empty except for a very smartly dressed elderly gentleman. Freddie gave the man a nod as if to say good morning. A barmaid came through to take his order – a small light ale. He sat down to wait. He wished now he had brought a paper. The elderly gentleman called over to him, "Would you come and join me young man, unless you're waiting for someone. But in that case, come over anyway."

"Thank you sir, I will." But before he could sit down the man gave him a ten shilling note and requested Freddie to order him a large whisky and to have one himself – a whisky that is. The man introduced himself as a Mr Brown from somewhere on the Oxfordshire Gloucestershire borders and stated that he was visiting his daughter for a few days. Freddie in turn told him about his life so far, his work, his time in the RAF and now back in civvy street, finding it hard to adjust and having a few problems which would not resolve themselves.

"Ah! to be young," the man interjected, "we have all been young. You keep looking at the door, are you expecting someone?"

"Yes, a real English young lady, very attractive and very nice." But before he could stop himself he blurted out that she was married.

"Oh dear." Mr Brown then said, "You are in dangerous territory. Be very careful. By the way, what's your name?"

"Frederick. My family and my intimate friends call me Freddie." By now more than an hour had passed and every time the bar door opened he would look up to see if it was her. In himself he kept making excuses for her. Perhaps she had not got the letter or she just for one reason or another would not come.

Mr Brown got up and said, "I must be going. Here son, here's my card. Give me a ring. I would like to give you a few tips about life in general. I expect you wonder why I am taking an interest in you. Well if nothing else I respect the RAF."

The gentleman responded whilst finishing his drink and getting ready to leave. He said:

"Will you permit me to give you some advice, Fred?"

"Certainly, sir, what is it?"

"Work for yourself, buying and selling – always make a profit, never at a loss!" And with a twinkle in his eye he said, "I hope the lady friend turns up!" They shook hands and Mr Brown wished Freddie luck and went on his way.

It was now twenty past one. He would have to leave soon, at 2 o'clock the Brown Bear would call time. By now it was ten minutes to closing time and still no Deborah. When he was preparing to leave, as on the station platform, there was a tap on his shoulder. It was her.

In spite of the crowded bar they unashamedly embraced.

"Let's go," she said and at that moment the taxi driver got out of his cab and shouted to her, "Oy, what about paying me Mrs?"

"Oh, I'm so sorry, Cabbie. Here, keep the change." What note she had given him Freddie could not discern, but the cabbie said:

"Thanks, love, you can ride in my cab any time," and waved to both of them. After repeatedly saying sorry for leaving it so late in arriving, he was forced to mildly rebuke her, saying:

"It doesn't matter, you're here now."

Freddie suggested they walk up into town and have something to eat and drink. He particularly wanted a cup of black coffee as he was beginning to feel the effects of the brown ale and the three whiskies he had drunk with the gentleman in the Brown Bear. They set off and she held him in a tight grip, arm-in-arm in a lock as if she was his prisoner. On settling down he asked her what all the urgency was about. She told him that she had had some bad news regarding their friendship. Rebuking her again he asked, "Is that all we are Deborah?"

"No, no, no, darling, you know I love you. I'm finding this very hard to say."

"Well don't beat around the bush, out with it."

"Well OK then, here goes." She lit two cigarettes and gave him one of them. "You see, when Maurice left the Staff College he was given some leave which he spent with me at my parents' home and three days ago an official letter was delivered by hand by an RAF officer. The letter informed him that he had been promoted to the rank of Group Captain and subsequently been posted to command an RAF operational station in West Germany. Now here comes the worst bit, Freddie. He insisted that I go with him and I gather the RAF do as well. So dearest, I see it as my duty to go with him. Do you understand?" A tear trickled from one of her eyes and holding his hand, she explained, "I'm so sorry, but I have no choice but to go. This has been an uncomfortable week at my Mum and Dad's house. Daddy and Maurice don't get on at all and sometimes the air is thick as fog. Now Freddie, the time has come for me to go but before I do could you do me a great favour?"

"Yes of course."

She interjected with, "You do love me, don't you?"

Now it was his turn, "Deborah, haven't I proved it to you since our time in India. Why do you ask questions like that?"

"I'm sorry, I don't know what I'm doing over all of this mess."

"Well before I agree to do you this favour, do you love me and I want a straight answer."

With no hesitation she said, "Yes I do. I adore you. I would marry you tomorrow if I could. Sometimes I am physically sick. My mother keeps thinking I have fallen for a child, which they would like, but it is the thought of you." By what she had just said he was completely disarmed. His mouth trembled and she noticed this and realised that in reality whatever the situation they would be inseparable. With that she leant over and picked up a paper carrier bag given to customers. He noticed she had two and they were identical. "Here darling, here is a parcel. Would you keep it in a safe place? I was going to put it in a Harrods' safe deposit box but on the way I sensed I was being followed and so it proved. She stopped when I did and twice I saw her reflection in a shop window, so I did more shopping and then I returned home. Do you think I was clever?"

"Yes, you were very clever."

Still holding the bag she said, "Also in here is a present from me to you and also one from the Group

Captain. I understand he gave it to you as a gesture and a thank you for saving his reputation when you cleared up after he had taken tablets and whisky. I proved I loved you, you see, I told him if he did not I would refuse outright to accompany him to Germany." Laughingly she said, "It's ironic when you come to think about it, but for the quick thinking of ACI Freddie Radnor, Wing Commander Churton is now a Group Captain." Still smiling she said, "I suppose that's life."

"Give me the bag, I will look after it for you. Now please leave right now, Deborah, as you are laughing and happy. Don't look round, just go. Someday we'll meet again. There, I sound like Vera Lynn. Off you go. I love you." Fortunately he was sitting with his back to the street so if she did look round he would not see her.

In the ashtray where they had been sitting there were two cigarette stubs side by side. Both had lipstick marks on, hers of course. A waitress came to clear the table but Freddie stopped her and picked up the two stubs and carefully placed them in his half-empty box of matches, for if nothing else the stubs came from her kissable lips.

He left the café feeling in a daze, and decided at a stroke to make for the train station, kidding himself that she would still be on the platform. Her train might be late. Briskly walking all the time, eventually breaking into a trot, he arrived on the platform. He looked left and right but it was empty. Near the ladies' waiting room? No, that too was empty. Suddenly a porter came up to him, and asked:

"Can I help you, sir?"
"Er yes, has the London train gone?"
"Yes, smack on time. Your lady friend got on it."
"How do you know she's my lady friend?"

"I've seen you both many times. She's a good looking girl and a figure to go with it."

He wished the porter had not made that particular remark. Then, he left and to kill time walked around window shopping. When he had had enough, he too went to catch his train back home. Only a few moments after he got on the platform his train came to a stop, but before this happened he had sensed that he too was being followed. He noticed there were only three other people boarding the train. As it pulled away he looked out of the window but no-one came late, so he dismissed it as nothing, but at the same time could not be sure.

Freddie sat down. He was lucky the compartment was empty except for an abandoned newspaper. But unknown to him, he was being watched right up until the last moment. He had made the journey so often by now he could not be bothered to gaze out of the window, so he picked up the abandoned newspaper and turned a few pages, pretending to himself that he was interested. He stopped, now he was very interested. There, staring him in the face was a photograph of AC2 Ginger Towner. The headlines accompanying the photograph read, 'Ten years for a safe breaker'. Freddie's heart raced like nothing on earth. This was the same man in his Flight in India and sometimes when the occasion warranted it he had been Freddie's co-driver. Things were now falling into place.

He soon arrived at his home station and in his excitement he nearly left the carrier bag. Again he had got himself into a frenzy. When he got home he went straight to his room and opened the parcels and letters. The large parcel was sealed with wax – he knew what it contained. The next was supported by two sheets of cardboard – it was a studio portrait of Deborah. He quickly put it face down because he could not bear to look at her. In the next was a very expensive fountain pen with a note 'To the love of my life' and signed 'Yours forever, Deborah'. To him it was the first time in her own way of giving him permission to always address her that way. The next envelope he opened was cold and official. It was from the new Group Captain Churton, briefly thanking him for his time as his official driver in India and as a reward the Group Captain had enclosed four £5 notes. It was for Freddie more than a month's wages. And now to the last one – he knew it was from Deborah.

  The envelope was rose red. He did not open it as he had done with the others. Instead, with his thumb he gently prised it open so as not to damage anything. The first thing he took out was a letter in which she said how much she loved him and apologised for not taking their friendship to a higher level. At first this last remark puzzled him but soon he realised it was referring to the fact that they had not consummated their love. She added that the reason was she had to be careful. He was now happy. From the red envelope another one was retrieved and he repeated the same procedure, opening it with care. There was no letter but a money order for £40, also a £20 gift voucher to allow him to shop in Harrods. With this he broke down and had to go for a walk.

CHAPTER 15

Freddie went looking for work, which he needed before completing the last remaining year of his apprenticeship. One firm did not dismiss him out of hand but told him to come back the following week when the boss would be back from a conference. He thought, well there's a chance and went home. His mother made them both a cup of tea and they were sitting down together when there was a knock on the door. His mother, as usual, answered it. On opening the door there stood an RAF officer who asked if a Mr F.W. Radnor was in? She called Freddie and, to his surprise the officer was a Squadron Leader. He asked Freddie for his pay book, assuring him it was to make sure he had the right man. Freddie got it and the Squadron Leader then handed him a large box. The officer remarked on how heavy it was – too heavy to send by post. The Squadron Leader said he had had it for three weeks and this was the first opportunity he had to deliver it. It was pleasantries all round and Freddie's mother asked the officer if he would like a cup of tea.

"Yes I would," he answered, and was invited to sit down. Neither Freddie nor his mother knew how to speak to their guest but he soon put them both at ease by telling them that his name was Thomas, but "please call me Tommy." He then said, in between drinking his tea, that the box was from Mrs Churton, with fondest regards from the Group Captain and herself. Finishing his tea, Tommy said he had to be on his way back to Northolt Air Station. He wished them well and off he went.

Freddie and his mother had a race between them back to the box – it really was big and heavy. But Freddie had to remind his mother that it was addressed to him. On opening the box, inside were tins and packets of food, some of it they had not seen since 1940. Tins of fruit from South Africa, meat from Australia – something for every occasion. But to his dismay as he was unpacking, Freddie realised there was no letter for him. That is, until right at the bottom there it was, from her to him alone. And this time it had not been opened. The envelope and the notepaper were red. He went to his bedroom to read it, it began:

R.A.F. Married Quarters West Germany 13th May 1948

My Dearest Freddie,
This box is for you and your family to enjoy as I know how difficult life is for everyone back home. It is about time this Government rewarded the British people for all they had to put up with during the war. I think of you every minute of the day and when we met and spent time together walking by the river and sitting in Ray Mead Island Park. Also that lovely day in Cookham when we passed Stanley Spencer pushing his old pram, then having lunch at The Ferry.
I am not very happy here in Germany, although on the Base we want for nothing, re the box of goodies for you. But it is India all over again, except of course it is colder. But it is getting me down. Whisky and cigarettes

help. I hope you have settled down in civvy street after your time in the R.A.F.

Squadron Leader Tommy Haldane who has delivered the box is my husband's P.A., but sometimes he flies from the base to Northolt, which is how I can be sure you will receive this. He is not unlike you and like you is a very good dancer. But don't worry, he is getting married in June. When I dance with him I imagine I am dancing with you. Well, I think that is all I have to say for now, darling. God bless you. All my love, and more.

Yours forever,
Deborah

After reading her letter in his bedroom and crying, he hid it with the others she had sent him. As he composed himself, he heard raised voices from downstairs. Wiping his eyes he went down to see what was going on. He could not believe what was happening. During his time upstairs some of his siblings had arrived home from work and on seeing the box and what it contained, one was having this and another taking that. Freddie let rip at all of them saying, "Put everything back in the box!"

In temper he took it to the shed out the back and nailed the top down, then brought it back and told everybody it would be opened when he was ready. He reminded them that the box and its contents were sent to him and him alone. They were all stunned by his anger and to them his meanness. In fact the whole episode from everyone's viewpoint had disrupted the family. After about half an hour things went quiet and no more was said. Freddie pushed down his tea then got himself ready and went out for the evening, hoping he would not meet anyone he knew. Solitude would be his friend. Where shall I go? To the pictures or a dance? He opted for the dance floor, taking his cue from Deborah about dancing with Squadron Leader Haldane. So he went to a dance. He was never short of pretty dancing partners and as a result his spirits were lifted by the time the MC announced this was the last dance of the evening. He returned home in a reasonably happy mood.

The next day he had to report to the Labour Exchange but there was nothing for him. Eventually he returned home, only to be told by his mother that two men had called to see him. Since he was out they had left a message to say one or both would call back at 3 o'clock the next day, to make sure he would be in. His mother said that they frightened her and enquired what he had been up to. For a moment he was stumped for an answer. All he could tell her was that they would have to wait and see. Conveniently it coincided with some disturbing news in the papers and on the wireless. Soviet Russia had suddenly stopped all rail and road traffic through the Russian Zone to West Berlin and so Freddie said it might be due to that, meaning he could be recalled into the RAF.

CHAPTER 16

The next day, promptly at 3 o'clock, there was a knock on the door. Freddie opened it and standing there was a face he had seen somewhere before. The man was invited in and they sat down in the living room. The atmosphere was cordial. The man asked Freddie whether he had had any correspondence recently from Mrs Churton. Freddie answered by saying very quickly, no, the last letter had been dated about late April or early May.

"If you like I can get it for you." When he returned the man grabbed it out of Freddie's hand and read it to himself very quickly.

"May I ask what you want, who you are and why you are interested in reading my personal mail?" The man apologized and asked him if he could take tomorrow off and come to this address. "Yes I can as I am unemployed."

When Freddie made that statement, the man's tone and voice abruptly changed to one of being surprised and sorry to hear it. "Well Fred, we will have to do something about that, as you are now one of us so to speak." He got out his wallet and gave Fred three £1 notes. He was assuming Fred was short of cash. "Here take this. You will need it for tomorrow, your train fare and all that."

"Thank you sir," Freddie responded and bid his farewell. After seeing whoever he was to the door, his mother immediately reproached him, wanting to know what it was all about.

"It's about the RAF. I might be recalled."

But still his mother would not let go. "You're in civvy street now."

"Well Mum, that's what I thought. I have got to go to London tomorrow." Arriving at the address in the Strand, he showed his pass and was met by the same man that had visited him the previous day. He shook Freddie's hand and enquired whether the £3 had been enough and Freddie said it had.

"Now look here, Fred, all of this is about Mrs Deborah Churton. When I take you in you will sit down in front of a large desk. Behind the desk will be five high-ranking officers from the Security Service and they will ask you some questions about your relationship regarding Mrs Churton. Just reply yes or no to begin with. Always remember you have done nothing wrong." Almost as the man spoke that word the door opened and Freddie was ushered in. Quite innocently Freddie put this five-man panel off their approach to him by asking, "What is all this about?"

Realizing this ex-RAF man had taken them aback, the one in the centre responded that Mrs D. Churton, the wife of Group Captain M. Churton had gone missing in West Germany. On hearing this most devastating news, Freddie fainted and fell to the floor. Upon reviving him and giving him a glass of water, it was suggested by the man in the centre that a short recess might be wise. Everyone agreed to this and, when the meeting was resumed, Freddie asked for details. At first the panel refused, but after conferring the man in the centre took over and stated that on the 24th of May Mrs Churton went with most of the officers' wives to the American

P.A. store. A head count revealed one wife was missing. The buses were delayed for over an hour while the whole building and surrounding area were searched, but to no avail. A full-scale alert was organized and an enquiry. Nobody could throw any light on the matter. The other wives couldn't remember Mrs Churton getting off the coach. It was as if she had disappeared into thin air. Nothing had been seen or heard of her for five weeks.

"Now young man, can you help us?"

Freddie was speechless. His reply was "No."

Another of the panel said that when they had searched her quarters everything was in order, right down to her clothes, cases, identity card and passport – everything was there that should be. "It is a complete mystery. The best brains are baffled!"

"May I ask how Group Captain Churton is, and also her parents?" asked Freddie.

"Well you can imagine they are frantic with worry. Tell us please, young man... try to think... can you throw any light on this matter in any way?"

"No, at the moment I cannot. I'm afraid that I am becoming confused and hungry." One of the panel suggested they break off for lunch and return at 2 pm.

The man who had called at Freddie's house ushered him into some sort of posh canteen where he enjoyed a good meal. At last the man introduced himself as Richard. Up until then only three names had been mentioned, the Wing Commander, his wife Deborah and his own. At 2 o'clock Richard showed Freddie into the room where the panel of five were already sitting down. After some pleasantries he was asked the same question, i.e. could he throw any light about Mrs Churton? He was asked when he had first made a personal encounter alone with her. Fred said it was a few days after he was introduced to the Wing Commander who had told him that the next day his wife had to go to the NAAFI store for something she required. He also told them about how she did not get out of the car as she was, in her own words, 'down in the dumps', but gave the Indian housekeeper a list of things to order. During the time in between, Mrs Churton had struck up not only a cigarette but also a conversation with him, by way of breaking the ice. After a month or so they had become friends and talked about quite a range of subjects. Freddie also told them that before he lived at the villa, when she and the Wing Commander went to parties, balls and receptions – and there were many of these – she always made sure food and drink were brought out to him. To him that was a nice gesture. But when, at the Wing Commander's suggestion, he had moved from his barrack-type quarters to their villa, he had the same food as they did. The cookhouse food for other ranks left a lot to be desired.

One panel member asked him to describe his new quarters. Freddie told the panel that there were two small rooms on the ground floor, all self-contained. He then added that it had been worth all the waiting about – what an official driver incurred on a daily basis.

"Did you see or hear anything unusual while you were there?" Freddie realized the panel, call it what you will, were stepping up the pace of their questions and it put him on his guard.

"Yes sir. One night I did hear some raised voices but I couldn't pick up who or what it was about." As the panel's grilling of him became more intense, Freddie's temper blew up and he shouted, "That's enough!"

These five nameless men were too much. They asked him if he would come back the next day and he said no.

Their final question was, "What is your relationship with Mrs Churton?"

He was so fed up that he told them, "We are in love with each other. It is not one-sided, it is mutual. You know that as well as I do. We both found out that we were being watched when we saw each other in Maidenhead nearly every other day when I was on demob. leave. So there you have it. Deborah and myself do not care. One day we hope to marry. So far as I am concerned, gentlemen, I have nothing more to say."

The one in the centre said, "Well, we have a lot to say to you, so as you are on our payroll and you have signed all the official papers, I have to order you to return here tomorrow at 11am."

At first the thought of once again being ordered about disturbed him, but he soon realized that he was employed by them so he had no choice.

Returning the next day, refreshed by an evening out and surprisingly more confident, promptly at 11am proceedings resumed. The man in the centre began by asking him whether he could think of anyone who might throw any light on Mrs Churton's disappearance. Not thinking, Freddie said that on the Saturday before she was flying to West Germany the following week, they had met up for the last time and had arranged to meet in The Bear in Maidenhead. But Mrs Churton had been delayed, arriving at about 1.57. It was unusual for her to be late and the landlord had said it was too late to take orders so they had gone to a café. There she had confessed to him that she did not want to go to West Germany. She wanted to return to show business but was put under a lot of pressure not only by her husband but also by the Air Ministry. She had told him that she only agreed to go to keep everyone happy, including her parents. It had been a long goodbye.

Freddie then stated that he had requested that he sit with his back to the street so that when she got up to leave she would not see him and he told the panel that he had not seen or spoken to Deborah since that day.

Nobody had anything more to say. The man in the centre asked everyone present whether they had anything more to say or suggest. Just as he was about to close the proceedings, Freddie asked permission to speak – much to their surprise!

"Yes you may speak. What have you to say, young man?"

"Well gentlemen, may I suggest that all present take a sheet of paper and without consulting write down what they think has happened to Mrs Churton. Everyone could put down all their thoughts and theories."

"Where did you get this idea from?"

Freddie said that during the monsoon season all the airmen in his quarters used to do this about any subject as it helped to pass the time. The man to Freddie's right thought it a good idea and asked whether there were any rules.

"Yes, each person is given ten minutes, sir."

"OK, let's give it a try, we've nothing to lose and something might come of it."

So paper and pens at the ready, at 12.05pm they all began.

Freddie looked up and was amused to see one of the panel guarding his paper by curling his arm around it, just like in school. This observation soon stopped and he got on with his own essay. After ten minutes Richard, who did not take part, called time and asked who would go first. Someone asked if they had a pack of cards and Richard said he did.

"I can put my hands on them, they are in the next room."

The cards were shuffled and all agreed aces were high, low reads theirs first. Our man in the middle drew a deuce. Freddie is next with a three, and so on. The man in the centre had a gut feeling that Mrs Churton had eloped with or had run away with another man – or perhaps that she was mentally ill!

It was Freddie's turn next. He had written down that loving and knowing her, Deborah had told him she did not want to go with her husband to West Germany because she disliked service life and wanted to return to show business; she had become very low and had had enough and had just walked out on the spur of the moment. But where and how far could she get with no papers, passport or identity card. Eyebrows were raised.

The next two had not written down anything, calling it all a farce. One said that they just didn't know. The last man agreed with Freddie to some extent, but added the proviso that he hoped she had not taken her own life. At this Freddie was visibly upset. The session was abruptly closed. Richard followed Freddie out of the room and said, "Don't leave straight away, go down to the canteen and get yourself something and then come back up to my office. I have something to tell you and some loose ends to tie up. It will be in your interests to come. Off you go."

When Freddie returned, Richard said, "I have been appointed to be your link man so in future always contact me first about anything to do with this department." He gave Freddie a 'phone number to ring and said, "We will also be in contact by mail. Do you understand, Fred?"

"Yes sir, I do."

"Good, well that's out of the way. Now fill in this form and I will help you. Don't worry, it's for your expenses."

When it was completed, Freddie thought it was a bit high.

"Don't think about it, it's all above board." Richard showed him to the door but stopped him going through it. He said, "Tell me Fred, what do you think has happened to Mrs Churton – privately of course?"

"I think that if she is found alive she has had a nervous breakdown. Or if she is dead, probably taken her own life, and if she has, she is lying somewhere remote or at the bottom of a lake or river – but I hope not."

CHAPTER 17

On the Monday following the meeting in London, as he did not have to get up to go to work, Freddie was last down for breakfast. His mother presented him with a letter and remarked that the stamp had not been franked.

"If you can steam it off, Fred, it could be used again." This one had not been tampered with! When he opened it, it was from Squadron Leader Tommy Haldane asking Freddie to meet him, if possible, at Ealing Broadway Station at 11 o'clock the next day. He was to tell no-one and should destroy the letter.

It's Deborah, was his first thought. He wondered to himself if 'Tommy' had smuggled her back to England. This disturbed him throughout the day and into the night. The morning could not come quickly enough. When it did his excitement betrayed him. His mother was as inquisitive as usual and he soon put an end to it by telling her it was an interview for a job. He arrived early at Ealing Broadway Station and sat in the waiting room. After a while he noticed someone walking up and down on the platform past the window. He was looking for a man in uniform but Freddie got up all the same and went out to see. It was Tommy in civvies.

Freddie called out, "Here I am, sir," and Tommy was most pleased they had met up and shook hands. They both agreed that a pub would be the best place to talk and The Crown was nearby.

"Drinks are on me, Fred. What's your poison?"

"A whisky if that's OK."

"Of course."

They were in the saloon bar and it was empty apart from them. Tommy said, "I bet you're wondering why I want to see you."

"You bet I am."

"Well it's about that box of food I delivered to your house. Now if anyone asks you about it, tell them you know nothing about any box or, more importantly, we have never met. Use everything in it and burn the box. Do you understand, Fred?"

"Yes," Freddie replied, "but what's the reason?"

"Well apart from the disappearance of Mrs Churton, Customs made a spot check at Northolt and caught one kite with a lot of stuff. It's as simple as that, old chap. Also, I have been grilled by some committee about Deborah."

"So have I, sir. I found it very disturbing. Tell me, how has the Wing Commander taken it?"

"Surprisingly well. Did you know Fred, he's now a Group Captain?"

"No I didn't, sir."

"Now look here, Fred, you're not in the RAF now so you call me Tom, is that clear?"

"Yes, and thank you."

Freddie suggested they have another round of drinks – it was their third. Tommy said, "Your Deborah was drinking and smoking a lot." At this remark Freddie confirmed that that was what she did when things got on top of her. Tommy said, "Fred there is a clue in that remark."

"I know her, she could not take any more of the life she was living. Her husband was obsessed with the RAF, a life of moving about from place to place did not suit her. She told me she was very happy in Maidenhead and she felt settled. But of course it could never be as the wife of a career serviceman. I would like to think she has just walked away from it all, but where to, Tom, is anyone's guess."

As they got up to leave Tom said, "Let's hope that is all she has done." With that they shook hands and went their different ways.

Arriving back home there was the usual, "Where have you been?" from his mother. What with no news of Deborah, things were beginning to get him down and he still used the same pretext that he was looking for work. He had his tea and went out for the evening.

On the Saturday morning a mate of his wanted a chippy for the day and this made a welcome diversion for him. But on arriving home there was a letter on the mantelpiece and the envelope was all too familiar. On opening it he found it was from Richard asking him to come to the same address as before on the following Monday. It raised his spirits, hoping they had news about Deborah. He wondered over the Sunday, but it did him no good at all. That Sunday was a beautiful sunny day and after dinner, on a whim, he decided to catch the train to Maidenhead.

When he arrived he took a bus to Boulter's' Lock and decided to retrace where they both used to walk, holding hands and more often than not arm-in-arm. But before reaching Ray Mill Island he got off the bus a stop short so that he could walk past the house where she and the now Group Captain had lived. He wished he hadn't, but never mind, and he proceeded to Ray Mill Island Park. He covered all the places and retreats and at the end of it all he sat himself down on a bench where he was able to witness the Thames tumbling over the weir on its journey to London and the sea. Reflecting on life's journey, suddenly a voice said, "Hello young man, where's your lady friend?" As he looked up, standing there was a very good looking lady, beautifully made up and dressed just like his Deborah. She repeated her enquiry and at the same time sat down beside him, telling her dog to stop yapping.

"I'm afraid she has gone away. Whether I shall ever see her again is in doubt," Freddie replied.

"Oh I am very sorry. Are both of you in love?"

"Yes we are, very much."

"Well then you probably will." This lady intruder into his solitude was perhaps in her mid-fifties. They exchanged a few pleasantries and she bade him goodbye. Freddie thought no more about it.

It was Monday again – now he asked himself what was he going to do? As usual he went to the Labour Exchange and this time they had a job for him in a factory which made roof struts for pre-fabricated buildings. When he went there to be taken on, to his horror it was simply banging nails into wood, which in turn was placed in a prepared jig. Any fool could do it. In the second week the foreman told him that the company had been undercut for a new contract and as a result unless some other work came in he would be sacked. But after hearing this news he said to himself, who cares?

On arriving home that same evening his mother went to the mantelpiece saying, "This came this morning." He knew it was from London. It briefly told him to ring the usual number to make a date and time to be at the office. During his dinner hour the next day he 'phoned from a call box outside the factory and Richard asked if he could make it the next day, as it was doubly important. So Freddie agreed – same time, 11 am.

He wasn't sorry. This job he had was so boring and repetitive. Of course he should have been at work, so he had to take the day off – sod the job, banging nails in all day he thought to himself.

On getting up the next morning and to fool everyone, he had to go to London in overalls. When he got to the Strand three hours early, Richard had to hide him out of sight. Richard looked after him well and when 11 o'clock came he was ushered into another room and met three men he had not seen before. They got down to matters straight away. Richard started by saying:

"These gentlemen have devised a plan for your future with us."

At once one of them said, "Tomorrow you will receive this letter I have in my hand. In this letter it informs you that under the government's ex-servicemen's scheme you have been granted a place at a technical college to complete your apprenticeship and then we will set you up in business. Your wages will be paid by a grant and the amount you receive must be kept secret. It will be paid by a money order and when you cash it, it will be best to use a large general post office so that the same person does not serve you or ask you questions. So how does that suit you?"

Freddie replied that he thought it a good idea. "I am very impressed; it will save a lot of explaining to my family and friends."

"Now there is something else which might not be good news." At this point the door opened and in came a man Freddie had not seen before. Richard introduced him as Doctor Noteby.

"Dr Noteby is here in case you faint or you are taken ill, because it has fallen upon me to tell you that the body of a woman has been found in a lake about twenty miles from the RAF base and the description fits that of your friend Deborah – Mrs Churton. Her husband has been flown back from leave to identify the body one way or another."

Freddie did feel a bit shaky at this.

The Doctor had everything ready for him – hot sweet tea, cigarettes, even brandy – but all Freddie asked for was silence to take in the news. On his way home he was in such a daze that he could not think straight. The only positive thing he could think of was that he must tell his mother so she would understand his actions and his behaviour.

When he did tell her, she cried for her son telling him that now she realized how much Mrs Churton, Deborah, meant to him.

CHAPTER 18

The next morning Freddie did not wish to get up or have any breakfast. So worried was his mother that she sent for the family doctor who arrived in the afternoon although it was a Saturday. The doctor said that he had no medicine for what was ailing Freddie and in his kindly way he encouraged him to get up and have something to eat.

The doctor's manner did the trick and Freddie got out of bed and washed and shaved.

With a warm handshake, his mother thanked the doctor and bade him farewell.

Suddenly, she remembered that a letter had arrived that morning and quickly gave it to Freddie. Of course, he already knew what it was – the letter informing him that he had been granted an ex-serviceman's grant to enable him to complete his apprenticeship and also a course in upholstery if he so desired. He broke the good news to his mother.

"There, son, life is not all that bad, is it?"

This ruse stopped all the questions being asked for at least the next six or seven months.

The following Monday, Freddie enrolled at the Technical College near Slough as he could get there by train and by bus. He was somewhat dismayed over this as the train passed through Maidenhead, constantly reminding him of Deborah. It was pointless worrying about it. Sometimes, when the train stopped there or passed through, he made out he was asleep.

After a couple of weeks, he was quite enjoying himself. He liked everything about the course and so did his mother as he was able to get a hot meal at lunch time.

On the third week, the head asked him to come to the office. When he got there Richard and another man were waiting. Richard said that the woman found in the lake was not Mrs Churton, although Group Captain Churton was only nine out of ten sure the woman's gold ring was not the one he had given his wife. Here the other man took over.

"Tell me, Mr Radnor, when you met and talked to Mrs Churton, did she ever say anything about politics or anything of that nature?"

"No, not really, our conversations covered quite a range of topics. Why do you ask?"

The man thought and hesitated before saying that, as all of her papers, i.e. passport, etc, had been left on her dressing table, she could not get far without them, and a more sinister motive might explain things. Freddie, not knowing who this man was, said:

"Such as, sir?"

"Well, it is a possibility that she may have held Communist sympathies and has defected to the Russian zone. It is not unknown, young man. She does come from a working-class background."

To say that Freddie was surprised at that last remark would be an understatement. 'Here we go again,' he thought – rank, class... everyone labelled, everyone and everything in its place. Freddie even began to wonder whether the war had been worth all the sacrifices that people had made. And even now, in 1948, they were worse off than in the War. The man who said about a possible defection to Communism quickly drifted away, leaving Freddie alone with Richard, who said it was quite likely, unless something else turned up. His last remark to Freddie was:

"I'll keep in touch – probably here in the college."

He liked everything about it and so did his mother as he was able to get a hot meal at dinner time. On the third week the head asked him to come to the office. When he got there Richard and another man were waiting. Richard said that the woman found in the lake was not Mrs Churton, although Group Captain Churton was only nine out of ten sure the woman's gold ring was not the one he had given his wife.

Here the other man took over. "Tell me, Mr Radnor, when you met and talked to Mrs Churton, did she ever say anything about politics or anything of that nature?"

"No, not really, our conversations covered quite a range of topics. Why do you ask?"

The man thought and hesitated before saying that as all of her papers, i.e. passport, etc. had been left on her dressing table, she could not get far without them, and a more sinister motive might explain things.

Freddie, not knowing who this man was, said, "Such as, sir?"

"Well it is a possibility that she may have held Communist sympathies and has now defected to the Russian zone. It is not unknown, young man. She does come from a working-class background."

To say that Freddie was surprised at that last remark would be an understatement. Here we go again he thought – rank, class... everyone labelled, everyone and everything in its place. Freddie even began to wonder whether the war had been worth all the sacrifices that people had made. And even now, in 1948, they were worse off than in the war. The man who said about a possible defection to Communism quickly drifted away, leaving Freddie alone.

CHAPTER 19

It was now mid-summer and Freddie was enjoying himself. He liked the college as it was far better than working in a workshop or a factory. His personality and manner were accepted by everyone. But on the horizon, the summer break of six weeks was approaching and he was pondering what he would do. He need not have given it a second thought as one day in July Richard came to the college, accompanied by an elderly man who was not particularly presentable. Richard introduced him to Freddie as Mr Cholsey and he would be taking Freddie under his wing during the summer break to teach him how to operate as a second-hand furniture dealer. They would be buying and selling and going to sales. He would learn how to price houses and items so that when they set him up in that business he would have some idea how to go about it. By now Freddie was enjoying life. Since he was a teenager when, money permitting, he would go dancing, to the pictures or theatre, but particularly the music hall.

The college was shutting down for the summer break. He and Mr Cholsey got on well together, as did Mr Cholsey's wife. They both told him he could have a room to sleep in if they got back from anywhere too late.

Deborah was fading into his past. On the journey back home, the train stopping at Maidenhead never bothered him now and as for the area surrounding the town, that too was in the past. One day Mr Cholsey said, "We're going to a government surplus auction at Great Missenden today, Fred. I've picked up some good stuff there in the past. You never know what you may come across."

On the day of the auction at Great Missenden, Mr Cholsey told him to get to the yard as early as possible before 9 o'clock as an early start was essential. Arriving there, Freddie was amazed at what he saw. They split up and arranged to meet at a certain point. He was advised to look at the vehicles as he would have to use a large van when he had his own shop or yard. Going along the rows and rows he came across lines of wartime cars, most of which were the colour of khaki. Except one. It was none other than an ex-RAF Humber Snipe, still painted in the distinct RAF blue. From the outside it was in good nick. The door was locked so he went back to the office to make enquiries about it.

The man who spoke to him said, "It has been there some time now but it's never received a bid. But to get rid of it you can have it for £25." He gave Freddie the keys and said, "No-one could start it up, but in any case everything that's auctioned is bought as seen."

No matter, Freddie thought. In his naivety, Freddie made the auctioneer an offer, but was told that every item of government surplus must be sold by a bid. He scoured the catalogue for its number but it was not listed. By now the man was getting bored by this young upstart and in a temper, much resembling a Flight Sergeant's, told him to come back at the next auction and take his chance against a bidder. Mr Cholsey had heard the commotion and asked Freddie what it was all about.

He just replied to him, "That's your first lesson. We will come next time. What do you want the car for,

Fred?" Freddie said that he had driven one in India and liked them. "Well, it's your money, but if you're successful in your bid let's hope you're not buying a pig in a poke."

"I don't think so," he replied.

On their return home, Mr Cholsey said, "I know we haven't known each other long, Fred, but in future call me and the wife Charlie and Gladys."

Freddie thanked him and said, "I'll try to remember. Tonight before I go home we'll go out for a drink shall we?"

"No Fred, I've got some indoors, then the three of us can have one. You get yourself home." On arriving back at Charlie's yard, Gladys told Fred that after he had left for the auction she had had a 'phone call from Richard for him. All he said was, "Tell Fred to report to the Strand as usual tomorrow morning."

Freddie replied, "OK," adding what Charlie had said on the way home. "I have to call you both by your first names."

"Yes Fred, it was my idea and I told him to tell you." All three drank to that. Freddie was the son they never had.

Next day, Richard was waiting at the entrance to the office. "What is it this time Richard?" asked Freddie.

"Well, you have made it into the ranks, albeit at three up from the bottom. You will be doing mostly courier duties, so today you will be given a passport in your real name and a second one in a false name known only to us. So to begin with we shall want three passport photos. I will tell you about the third later, so follow me and we'll do the photographs first." All done with by the afternoon, he was told to use his genuine passport at all times, unless told otherwise. The third one was different from the other two.

"This one is for if you need to act quickly. Just show it and it will get you anywhere. But tell nobody about it, only those who need to know. Conceal it in the lining of your clothes. Give me your jacket and our tailor will do the rest." Freddie was most impressed and while the tailor was busy doing his task, coffee and sandwiches were brought to him. By mid-afternoon he was set up and ready for any task. On the journey home he sat in the train compartment feeling very pleased with himself. Although nothing was mentioned about Mrs Churton, it never entered his mind to ask and he left it at that.

It was now mid-September and everyone seemed to leave him alone. To all intents and purposes he was just an ex-RAF serviceman completing his apprenticeship at the college. He was content at that. Going out in the evenings dancing, the pictures and all the things a young man does. He had a few one-night stands to relieve sexual frustrations. Life was good and on top of all that, a money order every week – what more could Freddie Radnor want? What he did want above everything else was to know the fate of Deborah.

It was now late September and still there was no news. It seemed to him at times that she had just been a mirage. Had she fallen for someone else and eloped or both of them just run off and taken new identities? At that time in Europe there were plenty of displaced persons and they or she could have mixed in anywhere. Freddie broached this with his controllers and they in part seemed to agree. But as soon as someone put forward a view, someone else killed it off. He was told to just forget it. Perhaps they are right, he thought to himself. Any mail he received had been tampered with. If they, the S.I.S., had not shown him how it was done he would not have been any the wiser. He was still not totally trusted by them.

CHAPTER 20

On October the 2nd, on arriving home from college, Freddie noticed a registered letter addressed to him. It was the first one he had received in his life. His mother remarked that she had had to sign for it and that it must be important. Before opening it he turned it over to see who it was from. It read, Mrs N.A. Cann, 93 Norton Square, London W.1. The name baffled him. He took the letter upstairs to open it and inside were two sealed envelopes, but they were wrapped in a folded sheet of notepaper. On the outside it read, "Please Mr Freddie, open number one first, then the second."

Quickly he followed as instructed. On reading its contents he became very excited. It began:

Mrs Noor Cann
London
1st October 1948
Dear Mr Radnor,
Your friend Mrs Deborah Churton has been in touch with me and has asked me to forward to you the second letter enclosed by registered post so that she can be sure you and no-one else will receive it. She gave me instructions what to do and I hope for both of you I have followed them to your satisfaction.
Regards,
Mrs N.A. Cann

Freddie was in a state of disbelief. Here he said to himself was proof that all she had done was walked out on the life other people had made for her – from her husband, her parents and the Air Ministry – and she was having no more of it. He then opened the first of the two letters. It read:

Central France

Dear Freddie,

I feel very guilty about what I have done, particularly to you and to my parents. As for the rest, sod the lot of them.
Briefly, when I left on that day at the American P.X, I saw my chance and took it. I could not take any more. Where I am and have been these past five months I have been very, very happy. I will tell you more if and when I see you. If you have found somebody else I will understand, but I hope you haven't. Accompanying this letter is what I would like you to do for me, if you possibly could. Please do not tell anyone where I am. Please do not betray me as I want to get out of this my way and that is with you and you alone. Please see separate letter marked D.

Love and kisses,
Deborah

The letter marked D read:

Freddie,

I realise you will have to obtain a passport and also to make some excuse for you will have to disappear for about a month, but please try for me. I know there are restrictions on the amount of cash you can bring out of England, but please bring as much as possible. Also you will have to get a visa from the French Embassy, then make your way to Paris and catch the 11 am train to Limoges, Central France, no earlier than the 10th of November. This train will arrive in Limoges mid-afternoon and from the 10th of November I will meet it every day for two weeks. Please come. If you do not then I will stay here as happy as I am.
    Yours forever,
    Deborah xxx

    What now? He thought to himself. Deborah had thought of everything, even giving him plenty of time to arrange their reunion. But where could he go to think? At first it was a walk, but it was getting colder outside so in the end he opted for the cinema and the most unappealing film he could find. In the cinema it would be warm and dark. Using all the ruses he had been taught at the training school for M15, he took with him a notepad and a pencil. He was off to the pictures. No-one could suspect anything unusual in that. Freddie left the cinema none the wiser. Then on the way home he decided on another ruse. He would 'phone Richard in the morning and ask that since he had been given the passports, was there anything he would have to do if he had to go, say, to somewhere in Europe? But he quickly changed his mind as it might arouse suspicion. In the end he decided to make tentative enquiries at the French Embassy. Here they were most helpful, except when he was asked why he wished to go to France. He had already thought about an answer if this question was broached and he told them that it was to bring back to England a friend who had been ill and wanted to come home. The visa section at the Embassy was most sympathetic and gave Freddie his visa and even told him the best way to get to Limoges. They told him to take the boat train to Dover and then on to Paris to connect with the train to Limoges. The whole journey would take up to about two days. He was also advised to spend one night in Paris so he would be fresh for the journey from Paris to his destination. Freddie thanked everyone, right down to the lady who brought in some tea, even though it left much to be desired as they hadn't boiled the water.

CHAPTER 21

Freddie left home on his journey on the afternoon of the 7th of November, saying goodbye to his mother and assuring her he would be all right. She made him some sandwiches in case he became hungry. He in turn gave her three one-pound notes. He was on his way. On his way to see his Deborah.

Arriving at Victoria Station he was informed by the booth that he should have booked in advance, particularly if he wanted a sleeper berth. But if he waited and he was a single fare he should get on the 9.15pm. His first mistake. But at 8.45 he was asked to return to the booth to buy his ticket and go to Customs & Excise for clearance. So far so good. He boarded the train and was shown to his seat. To him it was a strange experience but interesting. At the last moment a well-heeled lady sat next to him. Freddie opened the small talk by telling her it was his first time on the boat train. She assured him there was nothing to it and that everything was done for you. And she was proved right. The only thing he did not have was a sleeping place, so after supper he made himself as comfortable as he could. Time had caught up with him and he had not slept very well since Deborah's letter had arrived. During the night the movement of the train sent him into a deep slumber, but at some time he felt someone covering him with something cosy and warm. On awakening he found that someone had put a blanket over his sprawled out body. The train had come to a standstill. A waiter gestured him to the dining car for breakfast and it was most welcome.

Leaving the station he was in need of finding a room for the next night, but it must be cheap and near the station ready for his departure the next day. He sought out a gendarme who could understand English and was directed to a small hotel which was clean but very primitive. It would have to do. As he did not know Paris he did not venture very far from his lodgings. If ever time dragged it was here, all alone in this famous city. What was bothering him more than anything was that he had to watch his money. He was beginning to get annoyed at Deborah. Surely she could have come to Paris and met him there. She must have a reason why she did not. A cinema beckoned him so he went in, but of course he could not understand the film. All the same it passed the best part of three hours. As he left to make his way back to the hotel, someone said "Hello" from behind him. It was the same lady who sat next to him on the train.
"Where have you been young man?" He told her and also that she was a sight for sore eyes. She too had been to the same cinema. He grabbed what fate had thrown up at him and invited her for a coffee.
Without hesitating she said, "Yes. Follow me, there's a decent café nearby." They sat down at a table for two and began to talk. They exchanged names. "Ladies first please. I am Dorothy. And your name is?"
"Frederick, and to my mates it's Fred. To my intimate family and friends it's Freddie."
"Well to me you're Freddie. And whatever you do, do not call me Dot."

Neither of them could decide what to order. In the end it was a glass of wine. Dorothy enquired what time his train departed and Freddie said, "11 o'clock. It gets me to my destination mid-afternoon." He was too reticent to tell Dorothy that Limoges was his destination. They were the last customers in the café and the proprietor came to their table and informed them that he was closing and gestured with his right arm towards the door. Dorothy insisted on paying as she spoke near fluent French. Outside the café Freddie thanked her for her company, saying that if they were to meet again he would reciprocate the pleasure she had given him.

"Good night and thank you for your company," he said again. Going back to his grubby hotel Freddie felt much better in himself. The night passed, but Freddie was awakened by some loud noise – what it was did not matter. This is the day, he said to himself. Let me get ready and leave this dump of a hotel. He gave the key to the hotel proprietor then sought out a café for some breakfast, but there was nothing open. He had to keep asking people if they could speak English. Eventually someone could and pointed him to a bakery and what was on offer was not much to his liking, but when you're hungry you will eat anything.

His first impression of France did not impress him. The train arrived in Limoges and as it slowed down to stop he was already looking for her. Leaving the train, he stood looking up and down the strange station. Why hadn't they got traditional platforms? He was facing in the same direction as the train when a voice said, "Hello Freddie." He turned round and it was her. At first he did not recognize her, but all the same they put their arms around each other and buried their heads in each other's shoulders for goodness knows how long. Freddie wanted to let go but Deborah would have none of it.

She muttered, "Just hold me like you used to."

He was putty in her arms. When they did break apart, Deborah stood back and said, "Let me have a look at you."

Freddie in turn muttered, "Never mind me young lady, what about you? Where is your lovely long blonde hair and you have no make-up on."

Deborah retorted, "Where I have been and where I am now, I have no need for either." She asked him how he was and he said he was cold, tired, dirty and hungry. He asked whether there was anywhere nearby where he could get something resembling a cooked meal. Deborah said that the French eat differently from the English but that she would get him something. They walked a few yards and boarded a single-deck bus. She knew where she was taking him, but he had no idea. About ten minutes into the journey they got off the bus in some sort of market square and approached a café, but when they got to it that was closed. No matter. She led him round to the back door, opened it and introduced him to Madame Dupont. Deborah held his hand and told Madame Dupont what her friend from England required.

"Sit down darling, Madame has something for you." When it came, he asked what it was. Deborah said, "It is the French version of a stew, containing beef and vegetables, accompanied by a stick of French bread." Whatever it was he scoffed it down and felt better for it. He thanked Madame Dupont. It turned out that Deborah lived and worked on the premises. Debbie, as she was now called, showed him where they would be sleeping, but Freddie baulked and said no. Deborah pleaded with him, "Just for tonight, as we must watch the money." Freddie then agreed, but to him the place was a hovel.

After another meal at the café, he was shocked again when the café opened at 6.30 in the evening. He was hoping she would be sitting with him but no, she was waiting at tables. In his mind he was considering his options. After many cups of coffee, he knew what he was going to do the next day. The café closed at 10.30 and not a moment too soon. She had to help clear up and Freddie thought the whole thing was degrading and in their room he told her so. She began to cry but he consoled her. Deborah got into her bed and he did the same. The room was cold so Freddie only half undressed. They both said goodnight to each other, but there was no darling or sweetheart. Her oil lamp was extinguished.

Sometime around two o'clock Freddie could take no more – he could not sleep. Through his mind he called Flt Robertson, the man who had started all of this, all the names he could think of. He got out of bed and lit a cigarette, but this woke Deborah. Lighting the oil lamp she asked what the matter was. He tartly retorted that it should be obvious.

"I cannot get to sleep and I am bloody cold." She invited him into her bed, saying as he got in beside her, "I'm so sorry Freddie, cuddle round my back, I'm quite warm. Come on, we can't do anything, we've got too many clothes on."

He leaned over to kiss her on the cheek and they both settled down for what was left of the night. Some noisy activity outside awakened them both. Deborah turned over and kissed her Freddie for the first time in a bed. He thought that was nice, but the drab surroundings of the room soon brought him to reality. He opted to go first to wash and shave, but there was no bathroom as such, only a wash basin and cold water. This was the limit as far as he was concerned. Gathering his coat and case he told her to meet him at the railway station in three hours' time, which would be 11.30. Deborah shouted out:

"Don't leave me Freddie, don't leave me."

"Well," he retorted, "be there!" and stormed off in a temper and Deborah did the same. When he returned he half expected her not to be there but she was. He embraced her and mumbled, "I love you." Releasing her he asked, "Do you know the best hotel in Limoges?"

"Yes, follow me."

CHAPTER 22

It was not far from the station and Freddie led the way to the desk and booked a double room on a nightly basis. He was loaded with cash and Deborah asked, "Have you robbed a bank?"

"No, I will explain when we are alone in our room." The hotel was quite a posh one and they were both looked upon with some suspicion. However, their money was as good as everyone else's and when they got in and looked around, Freddie said, "This is more like it." Deborah thought it was out of this world. She did not have much in the way of luggage and to her surprise the hotel provided two white dressing gowns and ample towels. Freddie suggested that the best thing for them both was a hot bath and Deborah responded, "You're a mind reader!"

She went into the bathroom and while she was in there he sat himself down in a reasonably comfortable chair, lit a cigarette and started to unpack his case. Half way into this task he came across the sandwiches his mother had given him and he laughed to himself because they were now inedible. Deborah called out to him:

"Freddie darling, would you come in please?" He did not hesitate and went in. There she was, splashing about as though she had never had a bath before. She said, "Be a dear and scrub my back." He rolled up his sleeves and she sat up straight. This movement exposed her lovely breasts but Deborah made no attempt to cover them.

While doing as he was told, he remarked about the colour of the bath water. "Blimey Deb, when was the last time you had a proper bath?"

"Back in May, that's when." He said he thought she should have another before they turned in and Deborah nodded, "Yes," adding there was some blood as well. Freddie knew what she meant. She said, "I will have to go to a chemist to get some towels."

"No, I don't want you to leave our room until I say so," Freddie told her.

"Why Freddie, why?"

"Well, I'll tell you after we have settled in and had dinner. I am having all our meals sent up by room service." She was amazed at how different he had become. Was something on his mind? Freddie suggested they send for a maid to go into Limoges and do some shopping for her, to buy her some clothes, if possible, or anything she wanted.

"Freddie, Freddie... where have you got all this money from? Where? Where?"

On going to have his bath he retorted, "I will tell you everything tonight and I would like you to do the same for me, darling." When he said "darling," she was reassured of his love for her. After his bath he got dressed and went down to the hotel desk and gave them instructions that dinner was to be brought up at 8 o'clock. He asked for the menu or what was on offer and took it back up to their suite. Deborah looked her old self by now, except for the absence of her long blonde hair, and he told her so.

She responded, "It will not take long to grow." Freddie asked her whether the money was bothering her and she said yes, it was.

"Well darling, here goes. I must go right the way back to India and the day I was appointed to be your husband's driver. But before I was introduced to him I was ordered to see a Mr Jones."

"Oh him," she said. "In short he told me to report to him every day if I should hear anything but anything from gossip to any other source and to tell him. I later heard from one of my mates it concerned a safe robbery, also smuggling jewellery back to the U.K. For a fortnight there was nothing and then you entered my life, when I drove you and the housekeeper to the NAAFI store. You did not get out of the car and I offered you a cigarette."

"Yes, I will never forget that day."

"Tell me Deborah, why was it two weeks before I drove you anywhere?"

"Oh dear, later, later. Carry on Freddie."

So he continued, "Well after our first meeting the next was when I drove you and Mrs Elison to that large house and after about three hours you both came out to be taken back to base and you were both ill. Mrs Elison stormed off and I dried you off as best I could."

"Yes, again I will never forget it. When you put your hands over my body I can tell you now you sexually aroused me and had Joan Elison not been there I would have helped myself to you. You were the first man to make me feel that way."

Freddie was flattered but went on, "After I drove you to the station hospital, I drove the car back to the motor section to be cleaned. As I gathered up my things, I found your handbag and also where Mrs Elison had been sitting were two gold medals. I then hid your handbag and put the medals in my pocket. I should have taken your handbag to Mr Jones as ordered, but I didn't. I opened your bag and found inside a large necklace. I think Mr Jones would have been very interested in that necklace, so as a result I let you off. If I had shown the bag unopened to Mr Jones, you would have been in trouble, big trouble Deborah – possibly imprisoned. He would have tied it in with the safe robbery. So there you have it, I was and am a member of MI5 or, if you like, an agent for the security service."

Deborah began to cry and got up from her chair and embraced him. He in turn gave her assurance that he was always on her side, no matter what, come hell or high water. Their talk was interrupted by a knock on the door – it was a waiter with their dinner. There they sat at an improvised table for two in a world of their own.

Freddie suddenly realized that Deborah could speak fluent French and he asked her when she had learnt. She told him she had been top of her class at school and all it needed was polishing up and working as a waitress these past five months had helped with that.

"You must teach me one day, it might come in useful in my job."

"Of course I will darling, and you can teach me to drive."

"It's a deal." After dinner, which they both enjoyed, Deborah suggested that they both have another bath, "Why not, it's on the British government," he said.

"By the way, what is that other strange-looking lavatory pan?" Deborah laughed and told him it was a bidet. "What's a bidet?"

"Oh never mind, it's mainly for ladies to use."

"Oh, I see."

They both retired to bed and he asked her how she had managed to get to Limoges without any papers or passport. She began to tell him but suddenly mumbled something and then stopped. She had fallen asleep. She looked happy and contented so he got out of bed, locked the door, put out the lights and got back in beside her. While doing all of this, he made up his mind what to do next. Above all he must take her to Paris and give her over to the authorities and bring all of this to an end, if only for the sake of her parents and her husband, the Group Captain. He cuddled round her back and he too drifted off to sleep, his mind clear of everything.

CHAPTER 23

Freddie was first to rouse up from his most memorable night's sleep. He got out of bed and rang down for room service. He also asked them to send up with the early morning tea his bill for the first night. When both came, Freddie was shaken to the core at the cost for just one night. The next thing was to see how much he had left. What he had to do was to add up as best he could the price of two tickets back to Paris. He had enough and some to spare. He poured the tea and took Deborah's over to her. She herself was just coming to and wished him a good morning and said, "Let me kiss you."

"Well sweetheart, we must make our way to Paris today as the money is running out." He backed up his decision by showing her the bill but Deborah sat bolt upright and said she would go down to the desk and query it. She quickly returned saying that every item was correct and that she had no choice but to go along with Freddie's plans. They both washed and packed their respective cases. As they went to close the door of the apartment they both looked back into it, thinking how happy it had been to have twenty-four hours by themselves. Freddie paid the bill and Deborah did all the talking in near-perfect French.

At the station, Deborah again did all the talking and told him they would have to wait about an hour. While passing the time he asked her how she had managed to get as far as Limoges without papers or passport. She said simply, "I rode my luck, but all the time I was hoping to get caught. I had no idea where I was going. I needed no food or drink, I just had to run and run to get away from it all. You, darling, never entered my head. Somehow I reached Paris and I found myself at the railway station helping two nuns trying to control about twenty or more children. Instinctively I helped them to their train and as it drew into the station I boarded the train with one of the sisters, while the other counted their charges. We had a carriage to ourselves and the guard did not bother to check. I put one child on my lap and cuddled it. I know what a cuddle means to anyone. I had no idea where their destination was. I spoke to no-one. I fell asleep, as did the little child on my lap, only to be awakened when we reached Limoges. I then offered my services to the two sisters, which they gladly accepted. It turned out these poor little mites were on their way to an orphanage – most if not all were war orphans. The little lad on my lap would not let go of me. At the orphanage he began to say something but no-one could understand him. Anyway, whenever we could, he and I always tried to be together. I asked the nuns if I could stay for a while as I liked the peacefulness of the countryside and they reluctantly agreed, but said that I must work and earn my keep. All of this time only speaking French, I said "Merci."

Freddie said, "Tell me more on the train as it is due in five minutes." Deborah bought the one-way tickets and they boarded the train, settling down for their four-hour journey.

Freddie started to quiz Deborah again but she retorted, "No more darling. I will tell you one day. I cannot get little Freddie out of my mind – that's what I called him, after you dear."

"How old is he?"

"About six or seven, no more. And I think he is English. One day soon I am going back to the orphanage to make sure." Freddie was beginning to get exasperated over Deborah. What would she do next?

On arriving in Paris, Freddie took over. He got a taxi, a pre-war Renault, and asked Deborah to tell the driver to take them to the British Embassy. At this she baulked and said no, but he insisted and grabbed her arm and told her to get in and stop protesting as it was the only way. When they got there, Freddie paid the driver before getting out because he wasn't going to risk her running off. Holding her hand, he was literally dragging her into the Embassy. Getting to the main desk he asked for someone with a reasonable amount of rank or authority.

After a few moments a tall, smartly-dressed Englishman arrived. Freddie asked his position or rank and he replied, "I am P.L. Curtney, the Second Secretary. What is your business?"

Freddie replied, "This lady is the missing wife of Group Captain M. Churton and I now put her into your care and well-being."

Freddie was amazed at himself – how he had managed this unrehearsed introduction, holding onto Deborah so firmly he was hurting her. When the news of her reappearance filtered through the Embassy staff from all departments down to the reception area, the First Secretary took over and restored order. He dismissed those who were junior and not involved and ordered his aide to inform Deborah's parents and her husband, then the Air Ministry and MI5. It was evident they knew who Mr Radnor was.

During the mayhem, Deborah noticed Freddie was being eased away from her but she was too smart for them, so she slowly got back to his side and held his arm by her two hands, one hand holding his upper arm and the other just above his wrist. The First Secretary and the Embassy Doctor started to pull rank, but no-one was going to part them. This is what was in their minds. The Doctor said he wanted to examine her but she wouldn't have any of it, telling him she was quite well. As for Freddie, he too could see what they were trying to do – part them! It was stalemate. The First Secretary then came back at Deborah more angry and forceful, saying, "You are stranded here in the Embassy because you have no papers, have you?"

Deborah retorted, still holding Freddie's arm, "Yes I have."

"Show me them," he said, as if she were a child. She produced a French passport and identity card. "There, you see."

"If that is so, why have you come here?"

Deborah replied, "Simply to let everyone know I am alive and well. Also, there is another more important reason." Deborah came back at him with burning eyes, "In the orphanage where I stayed and worked there was a little boy who stood out from all the other poor wretches. He is English, of that I am sure. He should not be there. If you do not investigate, I will do it myself." Deborah had played an ace and won.

The First Secretary walked away. As they both stood there alone, nobody came up to them to ask a simple question, such as whether they wanted refreshments of any kind. That is until a voice from behind said, "Hello

Mr Freddie Radnor." As he turned round, taking Deborah with him, it was none other than Dorothy – the Dorothy from the boat train, the cinema and the café in Paris; they had met the night before he left to meet Deborah in Limoges.

"Ah, so you were no casual passenger on the boat train, were you?" Deborah stepped in. "Who are you and what is this all about?"

Before Freddie could explain, Dorothy said, "We knew he was up to something so I was detailed to follow him. I'm glad I did as he was completely out of his depth. We gathered you were still alive, Mrs Churton, and as soon as he went to the French Embassy to obtain a visa, we knew you were somewhere in France."

Deborah was speechless, but Dorothy broke the silence by turning her attention to Deborah, saying, "I understand you are concerned about a child in the orphanage where you did some work and that he might be English."

"Yes, that is correct."

"Well Mrs Churton, I can put you at ease. I have been in touch with all the agencies and they are going to look into this, but I warn you it takes a long time. They have to be certain. Do you understand?"

"Yes, and thank you," Deborah responded. Deborah almost at a stroke took to Dorothy and felt not only at ease with her but secure.

She assured Deborah that the boy would be seen by the agencies soon and also that they had some English parents who, for one reason or another, would be contacted. It would take a little time but she advised her and assured her that the little boy would be seen by the agency soon and also that they had some English mothers and fathers who for one reason or another would be contacted. It would take a little time but they should let the Embassy get them both back to England.

Dorothy turned out to be not only sympathetic to Deborah and Freddie's love and devotion to each other but later in life became a true friend. Dorothy was not pretty like Deborah, but English to the core. Neither tall nor well coiffured, dressed in what would be described as the diplomat's uniform – a tweed two-piece suit. Freddie did not realise that during his time on the boat train and in Paris he had been in a safe pair of hands. Dorothy came up to them with news that Deborah's husband was on his way to Paris. Freddie said he thought it best if he left and returned home, after all he had completed Deborah's instructions to the letter. Deborah said no, no and became hysterical. The Embassy Doctor was summoned to calm her down. With not too much effort he persuaded her that her friend was not going away and advised her that in the interest of everyone Mr Radnor should not be seen around the Embassy but that he would only be in the district outside until she had spoken to her husband. Deborah reluctantly agreed.

She had realised it was her duty to see him. After everyone had had lunch, news came to Dorothy that Group Captain Churton had arrived at a military airfield about an hour's drive away. Dorothy and other senior staff decided that Mr Radnor should leave for home as soon as possible. Dorothy drew Freddie aside and told him. He unhesitatingly agreed, but requested some stationery to write Deborah a letter. They agreed to his request, but he returned to the Embassy dining room to tell her he would not be far away while she talked to her husband. She readily nodded her head and he leaned over her and kissed her on both cheeks, whispering:

"See you soon. Don't worry. I love you." Freddie turned around and as he was ushered out Deborah blew him a kiss. He returned the gesture and she gave him her saucy wink and a smile and waved her hand as if she knew it would be a long time before they would meet again. To placate Mr Radnor the authorities pulled out all the stops. They gave him the VIP treatment and got him onto a BEA flight back to England, even driving him to his home, his family and back to some reality of a normal working life, or so he anticipated.

CHAPTER 24

After a period of just under two weeks, nobody bothered Freddie. Cash was no problem as he had three money orders waiting for him, but all the same he continued to go to the technical college. Even there he was left alone. But one evening, on arriving home, there was a letter. On opening it, it was from Deborah's father, pleading for Freddie to meet him at the Claremont Nursing Home, to help his daughter Deborah as she was not eating and refusing to take any nourishment at all and he was most concerned about her.

The next day Freddie put his bicycle on the train and cycled to the Claremont Nursing Home, not far from Taplow Station. With no trouble he was shown into Deborah's room and there she was in bed fast asleep and it was only midday. She looked dreadfully pale and drawn. He was accompanied by a senior nurse who gently woke Deborah and, on coming round, she saw he was standing beside her bed. She was speechless, but true to form her first words were, "Hold me Freddie, hold me."

She would not let go of him but she had to in the end. She looked up at him and kissed him endlessly. When she settled down she asked for Sister Margaret or whoever was on duty first. A nurse came rushing in followed by Sister Margaret. "Please bring me some dinner. I'm hungry. Please," cried Deborah.

Doctors came in as well – to say they were puzzled would be an under-statement, but at the same time pleased for her. The cause of the improvement in her mood and returned appetite was standing by her bed: it was of course none other than the ex-official driver of Wing Commander Churton, Aircraftsman F.W. Radley.

When the news of his arrival got round to all concerned, from her husband right through to MI5, it became obvious that these two people were inseparable, particularly Mrs D. Churton. One doctor jokingly said:

"If I could put you, Mr Radley, in a bottle or in a tablet, I would make a fortune."

In those days the midday meal was called dinner, and Deborah ordered whatever was on the menu and insisted that the same be brought for 'my dearest friend'. Whoever was paying, they would have to lump it. She got out of her bed, put on her dressing gown and both she and Freddie sat at the small table – it was dinner for two. After they had dined together, Deborah became tired and requested help from the nurse appointed to look after her. Her last words to Freddie were, "Please come and see me every day." She could hardly get 'every day' out of her mouth as she drifted off into a sleep. The occasion had been too much for her. Her face exuberant with pleasure and contentment.

To reassure her he requested from the Sister some stationery to leave her a note that from now on he would see or write to her every day but if he failed to do so it would not be his fault. Sealing the envelope he put it in her hand and even though she was asleep her hand clutched it.

Freddie was true to his word. He had no difficulty in getting to her. What he wanted from Deborah was her account of what happened when her husband arrived at the Embassy after he had left for England. But still after five more days in the nursing home she was not strong enough to tell him. It would be only a short while after he sat with her that she would drift off into a sleep. But he would stay holding her hand for as long as he could. Deborah knew what Freddie wanted to know and she would tell him when she was strong enough. Every day when he had to leave her, walking along the corridor of the nursing home and in the train he asked himself 'what had happened in Paris, it must have nearly destroyed her.'

It was a week later that things began to happen from all quarters of his life. Since completing Deborah's instructions to the letter, every one left him alone. His wages from MI5 had not stopped but he had neither instructions nor a summons to London, so he left things as they were. Finally one day Deborah was ready to tell him, beginning with her arrival in India.

"Freddie darling, it was a mistake, mistake, mistake. What I should not have done was to join ENSA, but I did. Then I should not have fallen for the tall, handsome and dashing RAF Officer, Wing Commander M. Churton, but I did, and he himself was so persistent and I think in retrospect he wanted to prove to his fellow officers – probably even had a bet – that he could woo and marry me. It was six of one and half a dozen of the other. He even broke King's Rules and Regulations by not getting permission from the AOC, who was away. My wedding night was a complete disaster. I knew even then what a terrible mistake I had made. Maurice too admitted it, two weeks later, when he came back to the villa one night after another wild evening in the Officers' Mess. We both agreed that we must keep up a charade until at least the war was over, but he did at certain times hope we could make a go of it.

"When we are married, Freddie... oh, I'm sorry, I'm being presumptuous..." Freddie assured her that that was what he wanted himself. His response lit up her face. Deborah discarded her dressing gown and returned to her bed, again reassured of his love for her. Freddie kissed her and said, "Bye, bye, see you tomorrow."

CHAPTER 25

Freddie arrived at Taplow Station and he did not have to wait very long as by now he had got himself into a monotonous routine. He found himself a compartment to himself and sat down at an angle, looking towards the other side of the compartment. He told a fellow passenger what a cold day it was but there was no passenger there, and Freddie fell asleep, completely exhausted. The next thing he knew he was being gently shaken by a porter telling him, "This is Oxford, sir, the train goes no further." Freddie could not move a muscle nor open his eyes. He could hear much commotion and loud voices, but that was all. The next thing he knew his mother and father were standing over his bedside. A nurse sent for a doctor, who gave him a quick going over and said, "What have you been up to young man? You have been in this hospital for nearly three days." His mother answered for him.

"He's involved with a married woman, doctor. It's too long a story to tell you but that is the long and the short of it." The doctor smiled and assured everyone that he was only over-tired and that they would keep him in for a few more days, then perhaps he would have a spell in a nursing home. His mother enquired who would pay for all that. The doctor said, "The new National Health Service. It's all free now. They call it from the cradle to the grave."

"Oh, that's OK, then. Make the most of it son." His mother's words gave him something to think about. Had fate stepped in to shape his life? On the fourth day Freddie was allowed out of bed, but only to sit in a dressing gown. He enquired where his clothes were. His favourite nurse, who had taken over him, was on duty and when she came into his room, and after all the pleasantries, he asked her a favour: would she go and fetch his jacket as he wanted some items from it. At first she said no, as she had no authority, but he pleaded with her and she relented and brought it to him, What he wanted was Richard's 'phone number, to tell him his situation and where he was. As the nurse was tidying the room he went to the secret pocket where it was, noted it down and gave the jacket back to her.

"What is your name, nurse?" he enquired.

"It's Joan."

"Well, here is my jacket, you can take it back now. Tell me Joan, can I get to a 'phone?"

"Yes, but I will have to take you in a wheelchair."

"All right, would you do that, please."

"Yes, but I must get permission from Matron first." Permission was given and Freddie got through but Richard was not there. His secretary said she would pass on his message regarding where he was and what had happened. He thanked her and put the receiver down.

This small activity made him tired and he requested to be taken back to his room quickly. It was proof of how ill he was. Freddie was awakened by a cough. It was none other than Richard, who told him not to worry about anything. He also told him that Mrs Churton was being informed, adding that she had had a relapse, probably because Freddie had not been visiting her. "We will have to see what can be arranged. To me at least you are both inseparable."

It was now early December, the last month of 1948, and what a year it had been. Leaving the RAF, being recruited into MI5 and above all going to France to bring Deborah back home. What would 1949 bring? The next day Freddie was told by the Doctor attending him that he was being transferred to the same nursing home as his friend, Mrs Churton. He also warned him that when he arrived at the home they would be in separate wings, but they would be able to see each other for most if not all of the day, until bed or rest time, to say the least. That arrangement was almost unknown!

The next day Freddie was told by the Matron that he would be leaving by ambulance to be taken to the same nursing home as Deborah's. In the meantime she advised him to inform those concerned where he would be until further notice. Doing this small talk helped pass the time. Having completed his small task he fell asleep, only to be awakened by Matron, telling him that the ambulance had arrived to take him to Hazel Lea Nursing Home. This was where Deborah had been transferred. Richard also had arrived. It seemed that he or they (MI5) were organizing everything. Freddie said goodbye to all the staff at Oxford, particularly Joan who on shaking his hand had a tear in her eye.

Richard had followed the ambulance to Hazel Lea and he drew Freddie aside and said, "There Fred, you see by working for us we can look after you in every way."

Freddie responded by thanking him and MI5, ending by saying, "It seems to me you can do almost anything you want to do, anywhere."

"Yes, you're right old chap, and always remember that." Richard said his goodbyes and left.

Freddie was wheeled into the male wing and into his ward. No single rooms at this place he thought. He enquired when he would be taken to see Mrs Churton.

"All in good time Mr Radley. Let's settle you in first," said the ward sister.

"No, no, not later but now," he demanded. He had hoped Richard had stayed longer. After angry exchanges between anyone who wanted a row, he was more than a match and as they all relented from the doctors downwards, he was taken to a common room. There she was, gazing out of the window into a winter scene of bare, leafless trees, flowerbeds and evergreen bushes planted at random. Deborah turned her wheelchair around and there he was. They wanted to embrace but a member of the staff remained, while the others withdrew. Deborah told him to leave as well but he did not. But she ordered him to, whoever he was, and reluctantly he did so. They both looked at each other. Words would not come from either for what seemed minutes. Freddie manoeuvred his wheelchair alongside Deborah's so that they could look at each other, imitating a lover's seat where the two, instead of sitting side by side, they would be face to face. They held each other as best they could from sitting in wheelchairs. Deborah finally let him go and after some small talk she came out with language and a tone in her voice he had not heard before.

"Listen Freddie, I've had enough of this situation we find ourselves in. I have already started proceedings regarding my marriage. I have let it be known that I do not want to see or hear from my husband ever again and I have applied for the annulment of my marriage so that we can be together. My grounds will be very simple: they are that the marriage has not been consummated. In plain English, Freddie darling, I am at this moment 'virgo intacto'. I have never been intimate with any man. Does that surprise you, dear?"

He could find no words, or if he did they would not leave his mouth. All he could muster was, "Yes, it does. I am speechless." But when he did find the words they were, "Is that the reason you have never encouraged me to get close to you in that sort of way?"

"Yes it was. You see, dear, when I realised my mistake on my wedding night I had to keep myself pure to prove that it was true. Please wait a little longer. I promise you will be the first and only man who will touch me with my consent."

During their time in the nursing home they both had time to spare. Deborah wanted some answers to questions that were niggling her and Freddie in turn wanted the same in return from her. A pack of cards was on a table nearby. Freddie got a nurse to shuffle the pack for them, asking what game they were going to play. Deborah responded, "Trust." The nurse, after completing their request, left the room bewildered.

"Here we go," said Freddie, "ladies first and aces high."

Deborah said, "No Freddie, let's do it this way."

Somewhat puzzled by this he said, "All right, but I don't understand."

"Well, now for a start. It's about some things that have been bothering me for a long time, and one quite recently. First, what happened to the ruby necklace you took from my handbag when Joan Elison and I were taken ill?"

"Well, I hid it and was very lucky to get it back home where it is safely, hidden. You can have it back whenever you want it."

"Oh darling, I don't know what to say."

"Say nothing. But now you answer my question. Why was it that I never saw anything of you, let alone drive you anywhere or take you to the few receptions and parties with your husband until that first morning when I saluted you and you tartly replied, 'you don't have to salute me Airman'. So I gestured my hand to shake yours?"

Deborah's response was, "About three weeks before I met you on that fateful day for both of us, I had been taken ill. It was nothing physical but mental. In short I had a nervous breakdown. I was very tired. It was all to do with the lifestyle we were all living. Through a Princess Noor, who is one of my best and true friends, it was recommended by the doctors that a few weeks away from the station would do me the world of good. So her father, the Maharajah arranged for me, accompanied by the Princess, to visit his summer palace in the highlands where the climate is cooler. Freddie dear, it was such a wonderful experience: the English food and peacefulness. I went to church every Sunday, something I had not done for a long time. There I prayed for something or someone to get me out of my situation. My prayers were answered when you came into my life. It was you Freddie, it was you."

Deborah wanted to continue but she was stopped by the appearance of the Matron and the Doctor, who needed to know what arrangements they had made – where or how or what they both would be doing for Christmas. Deborah with no hesitation or even consulting her dearest Freddie said they would if possible spend it here in the nursing home. Also there would be no arguments among either parent. Also, most of all, it would be their first Christmas together.

Matron said flippantly, "What about presents?"

Freddie, "I have mine here." Deborah broke down in tears of joy. That was Christmas done and dusted.

The next words came from the Doctor. It was, he said, time to get both of them out of their wheelchairs as they had done their job in restoring mental well-being. "Now gradually we must get you physically back to normal by doing some gentle exercises to start with. You both should be ready for discharge in the New Year."

As the matron and the doctor left both shaking their heads the doctor turned round and said, "In all my years in this profession I have never met two people like you and probably never will, again. The only comparison I can think of or have heard is the Duke and Duchess of Windsor."

CHAPTER 26

With Christmas now only two days away, presents and cards were arriving at the nursing home for both of them in equal measure. For Freddie one in particular stood out from the rest. It was from Mr & Mrs Brown wishing him well, but also informing him that in his absence at the last auction in Mildenhall he had previously made a ridiculous bid for the Humber Snipe that he was interested in, so he took it upon himself to bid for it and had secured it for £22. When he told Deborah this she too was overjoyed.

On Christmas Eve the ward sister came into the common room with the last postal delivery. There were a few more cards for both of them but for Deborah there was a letter. It was obviously something official by the quality of the envelope which was sealed down very tightly, and to open it she had to request a knife. Opening it inside was another sealed envelope addressed to Mrs D Churton c/o the British Embassy in London 'please forward'. Somewhat momentarily puzzled by this she could not open it quickly enough. On reading the contents, which were in the most eloquent handwriting in English, Deborah suddenly ordered everyone including Freddie to leave. This was to say the least not only unusual for her to order him to do anything and at the same time she was bursting into tears. At first she had to shout at everyone again to obey her order so they did.

Freddie was last to leave the room. Her look to him in her eyes was 'sorry' but he read them as she intended him to do. Freddie stood outside the door eager to enter first. While he stood there he imagined the worst scene. Had the Group Captain done something to himself or at least attempted and failed. Time, for everyone in the corridor, stood still. It seemed hours but in reality it was only a few moments.

Deborah opened the common room door and said, "Freddie come in dear," at the same time apologizing to the staff and other patients, but those in authority put their foot down telling her it was not for her to say who should come in or stay out, so Freddie and Deborah walked arm-in-arm down the corridor. There she gave him the contents of the letter to read. It was this:

The letter's contents:

Dear Mrs Churton

It gives me great pleasure to inform you that thanks to your concern and compassion while serving as an assistant at the orphanage near Limoges and alerting the British Embassy in Paris the young boy you always believed to be English is the son my husband and I have been searching for since the end of hostilities in 1945. We are most grateful to you. Andreas recognized me and I immediately knew that he was our son. At the moment my husband is in hospital in the American zone recovering from his traumatic experience towards the end of this terrible war. Finding our son has helped in his recovery a great deal. In the New Year I will hope to meet you and to thank you personally. I will then furnish you with details how as a family we got separated. Thank you so much. We are eternally grateful to you. Best wishes for Christmas and the New Year.

Kindest regards,
Pamela Hulle

On reading the letter's contents Freddie's eyes welled up and looked at Deborah who had been put down by the Doctor, Sister and Matron because she had ordered everyone out of the common room. She had the twin looks of a schoolgirl who had been reprimanded and one of joy. Freddie said, "Darling how wonderful I am lost for words, you were crying in happiness at the outcome of your effort about the child."

He went over to her and embraced her whispering, "Is it any wonder I love you." Deborah and Freddie each had the best Christmas presents anyone could wish for. Their Christmas in Hazel Lea was the most pleasant and enjoyable they had ever had.

CHAPTER 27

Into the New Year 1949 Freddie was the first to be discharged from the nursing home followed two weeks later by Deborah. They both kept in touch anyway either could devise. In the meantime the annulment of her marriage was going through the various stages it had to, and as for Freddie he was waiting to be summoned to London and to find out about his future with MI5. When he did go all he was told was that nothing had changed and he was on their books and was told to carry on attending technical college as then they knew where he was.

In the meantime Deborah wanted to return to the theatre as a dancer but was turned down. Were they getting their own back because of her desertion of the ENSA company she left in India to get married? She made enquiries but was assured this was not the case so she went on the books of a theatrical agent, as she was still, in effect, a member of Equity. If nothing else she might get bit parts on the stage or in films. In February Deborah had to appear in person at the family division regarding her petition for the annulment of her marriage. Freddie was excluded from all of this. It was no concern of his, but the sitting judge was not satisfied that she was 'virgo intacto'. He did not believe her and ordered an adjournment. Also all parties including her husband and their respective counsels were to assemble in two weeks' time in his private chambers.

Deborah was shocked by this development but had no choice. She called the judge every name or object she could think of under her breath. The lady in her had taken leave of absence. When she told Freddie he too could not understand. That evening they both went out together, had dinner, then on to the 'Hammersmith Palais' to dance the evening away to forget their frustrations coming from all directions.

When the day of the hearing finally dawned everyone was assembled at the top of the elegant stairway first floor ready to be called in, herself, her husband, relatives and friends and of course Freddie who at first did not wish to be there but Deborah had pleaded to him to give her support. They were all called in by the court usher.

The clerk said, "The court will rise," and the judge appeared and proceedings began. No-one had the faintest idea what would happen. Deborah and her husband, who was dressed in civilian clothes, gave not a small glance to each other. No person other than those concerned were called, which were as the court's clerk read out their names, 'Mr & Mrs M.S. Churton and their respective counsels plus an independent observer chosen by the petitioner.

It seemed to Freddie that it was all over in a matter of a few moments in fact only five. The look on Deborah's face said everything. She was angry, pale and unsteady on her feet. She went straight to Freddie and asked him to take her to the nearest pub. "I need a brandy in fact two or three." They asked to be left alone and their wish was granted. When they settled down and Freddie had bought the drinks she told him what had happened in the judge's chambers.

"Freddie my sweet the judge could not and would not believe that our marriage had not been consummated and he could not give a verdict there and then. He ordered that I must undertake a medical examination to prove that I am still 'virgo intacto' so there is another delay for both of us dear." To Freddie it was incredible. He too was becoming annoyed and frustrated. Someone remarked to them, "True love is never an easy passage." It was none other than Dorothy. The three of them went to the nearest 'corner house' for coffee.

CHAPTER 28

When Freddie returned home that evening on that same mantelpiece, which since his return from India had held so much joy and disappointments he had lost count, now held another surprise. Freddie had no anticipation of what its contents would contain. Opening it while having his tea he saw it was from Richard. He asked Freddie to come to London at the above address at 12 noon for a routine meeting. As he was on their payroll he had no choice. Freddie had never been to the address he had been given. It turned out to be a large Victorian house in North West London. Richard was waiting in the porch to meet him.

"Hello Fred you've cut it a bit fine. Unusual for you."

"Yes," Freddie agreed, "I caught the wrong bus but here I am." He was shown into a room where three men were sat behind a large table, one of them he had seen before, the other two were new to him. He was invited to sit down in the chair provided facing them. As he did so the door opened and in came none other than Lt Col Hontas. Freddie thought to himself what's he doing here? As usual the man in the middle spoke first saying:

"We have some questions to ask you Radnor. This got straight up Freddie's nose thinking how about the Mr but made no comment. "Now young man are you aware that Mrs D.R. Churton has purchased a small terrace house in Maidenhead at a good favourable price to her for cash on the table?"

"No I am not, it is news to me."

"But she is your mistress is she not?"

"No she is not my mistress we are friends. I believe it is called platonic. But one day when she is free from her marriage we hope to marry."

"Are you telling us she has not told you?"

"Yes I am sir. What business or for anything else she does at this moment in time is none of my business and none of yours with respect, sir."

Here Lt Col Hontas intervened saying, "Oh yes it is particularly me as you may well know." By now Freddie was fuming replying to the Colonel:

"I thought I helped you solve the case with the ex aircraftsman in prison."

"Yes you did but some of the contents of the safe in India keep turning up – jewellery most of the time but also gold sovereigns like the one I gave you, do you remember?"

"Yes I remember and I still have it." Continuing he said, "As it is none of your business I would like to end this charade."

"Do not be impertinent young man. We will decide when to draw this meeting to an end."

Freddie apologized and said, "Are there any more questions you wish to ask me?"

After consulting each other the answer was, "No, you may leave."

Richard was waiting for him and had already composed a list of all his expenses for coming to London. On the list there were items that he would never have dreamed about so when he transferred them on to his expense form it came to quite a large amount. He submitted to the lady in charge of the department on the premises. He was given a money order and no query was broached.

On leaving the house bidding farewell to Richard he thought to himself, if he did not know any different, his expenses were cooked up to placate him as he had given them as good as he got. Freddie went into the nearest pub and treated himself to a double whisky and soda and seated in the saloon bar he pondered over various things.

It was true he had not seen Deborah so often these past weeks as she did appear to be busy, and then suddenly he remembered that today she had told him in one of her letters that on the 12th of the month she had been invited to the 'Ritz' in London to meet Mrs Pamela Hulle for lunch, who wanted to thank her personally for finding her son in Limoges. Realizing she might still be there he finished his drink and dashed across London. Fortunately, he successfully hailed a taxi. On telling the driver his destination the driver said, "That's a bit of luck mate I'm going there to pick up a gentleman."

Alighting right outside the main entrance to the Ritz, he thanked and tipped the driver, and then Freddie approached the commissionaire dressed in the hotel's livery. He then enquired directions to the 'restaurant' but the doorman told him he was not appropriately dressed and he asked to see someone in authority. A lady came to where he was standing, and Freddie asked her if she could go into the restaurant, and if there was two ladies one with blonde hair or the other one answering to the name of Mrs Pamela Hulle, to tell the blonde lady that Freddie would be waiting in Lyons Corner House as he wished to see her.

"Yes of course sir I think I can go straight to their table as Mrs Pamela Hulle has made the reservation. I am certain they are still there."

All of a sudden Deborah appeared, so excited she was still chewing some food. The lady who gave Deborah Freddie's message politely told her:

"Madam your conduct is not acceptable to this establishment. Please return to your table. The gentleman's note is there."

Deborah realizing what she had done apologized over and over again and said that it was the first time she had seen Freddie but could not hold or kiss him! It did not bother him because he was outside in the doorway. He was happily in his place but Deborah was out of her depth. She could have done that in India but not in a hotel, let alone the Ritz, one at the very top!

Later, walking towards Piccadilly Circus, the words rank and class swiftly passed through his mind and he thought it is better that way. He was also pleased with himself that he was not appropriately dressed so as to be allowed into the exclusive Ritz hotel.

When he got to the Lyons Corner House there was a queue waiting to enter; it was absolutely full so he waited outside for her. Eventually Deborah came into view. She was unmistakable even in a crowded street. He went to greet her but his greeting had to be restrained as another lady was with her. Deborah introduced him to none other than Mrs Hulle. Freddie shook her hand and said:

"I am very pleased to meet you and I'm so glad that you have been reunited with your son."

"Thank you," she replied and added, "well thank you again Mrs Churton, I must be on my way. I will keep in touch. Goodbye to you both."

In an instant Freddie disliked Mrs Hulle. There was something about her but as in the past he let it go. Deborah suggested they go to 'Swan and Edgar's' where they would talk, so arm-in-arm that is where they headed for. Deborah did not want anything to eat but Freddie did. It was now mid afternoon. The waitress told him, "All that is left is a cheese sandwich."

"It will have to do then and two coffees please," and off she went. Deborah at once asked Freddie what he was doing in London. He said, "They sent for me just to see how I was, that's all."

"Oh – them!" Deborah replied. "Are you happy working for that lot?"

"Well yes the money is very good and also I may, or both of us may, be given somewhere to live. You can't argue with that Debbie can you?"

"Er no no."

He had unwittingly set a trap for her. The waitress came to her rescue by bringing their order.

They both agreed to spend the rest of the day in London, Deborah waving a cheque from Mrs Hulle into Freddie's face as he was eating his stale cheese sandwich.

"This is what Pamela gave me on behalf of her husband and herself."

"Deborah's right hand thumb was covering the amount, not that he was interested. They went to a variety show at the 'London Palladium' then found an Italian restaurant where somehow the chef served them a good supper. It was the end of a very eventful day for both of them.

At Oxford Circus underground station they had to part – Deborah to make her way to Waterloo to return home to her parents with whom she had been living since her discharge from the nursing home, and Freddie to Paddington to do the same.

Parting was becoming more and more unbearable. They both decided to put a stop to this; they were acting as if they were two illicit married lovers so, by not meeting so frequently, it came down to just weekends.

This was much better as both could lead their own lives during the week. Deborah got herself a theatrical agent and surprisingly she was getting plenty of work as stand in and walk-on parts in plays; one of them to Freddie's amusement was as a magician's assistant. All she had to do was distract the audience while he did whatever magicians do. While getting back into show business it brought home to her that she should never have left it in the first place. To Freddie at last she was in a permanent state of happiness, as for himself he resumed his association with Mr Brown and learnt the tricks in and out of the actual business that he would one day be part of. The 'Humber Snipe' was also over halfway to becoming roadworthy.

CHAPTER 29

They usually met up on Saturday mornings to plan what they would do over the weekend. Nineteen forty-nine was now into springtime, a time of hope and new beginnings. On one such weekend they had arranged to meet in Maidenhead. They then took the bus to Boulter's Lock and strolled in Raymead Island Park. Suddenly Deborah sprang a surprise on Freddie by saying that during the past week on Wednesday she had gone to be examined to confirm she was pure, telling him, "It was more embarrassing than anything that had gone before in her life."

Swinging her around to face him he told her, "You were very brave," and kissed her, and then asked, "What happens now?"

"Well, all the parties concerned will be notified and then someone, the judge I think, will reconvene the hearing and again the judge if there is no objection will declare the marriage decree 'nisi' and set a date for the decree absolute. Once I get that date we can plan our wedding. My father will have his wish to walk me down the aisle a pure woman and give me away to the man I have chosen from many, which is you."

"When that day arrives, sweetheart, and you've been so patient, I promise I will reward you in many, many ways, each one with devotion and love."

Again he turned to face her, this time leading to just a simple embrace and by now attracting an audience in the park but they were both oblivious to the rest of the world.

The following week Deborah received news that the hearing for the annulment of her marriage would resume on the 15th of May at 11am, this added to her happiness. Her solicitor told her that it was usually quick as the divorce courts were very busy; it was he said the result of servicemen returning home after the war only to find their wives had been unfaithful in their absence.

To Deborah it came as no surprise after what she had witnessed in India and since her return to England. She asked Freddie if he would he be in the court on the day.

His reply was, "If I can," remarking, "it is your day Debbie, but I will try."

She also requested that from now on he should call her Deb or Debbie.

Freddie was, in fact, determined to attend the court but he wanted to distance himself from it all, but at the same time not to distract her or make her nervous by being there. He would see her when it was over. Freddie left it to the last moment to enter the court choosing to sit in the back row. There were not many people in the courtroom, not even her parents. From his position he could see the back of a head he thought he recognized. It was none other than the head and shoulders of Deborah's husband, the Group Captain himself. Seeing him was the last thing Freddie wanted to do. Also there was a very young reporter probably on his first assignment from a provincial newspaper.

At 11 o'clock the judge entered the court, the clerk saying in a loud voice, "The court will stand." The judge sat down; everyone followed. Freddie was fascinated by the procedures as it was the first time he had witnessed anything like it. The formalities over, Mr Justice Elderfield declared, "That the marriage between Maurice Wilton Churton and Deborah Jane Barker I declare null and void owing to neither of the said parties having consummated the union. Therefore a decree nisi has been granted immediately and the decree absolute will take place on the 14th June 1949. Does anyone in this court have anything to say?"

The clerk looked around and nobody said or gestured anything. The judge said the hearing was over, but before he put this into practice he asked for Mrs Churton, accompanied by the two barristers, to go to his private chambers. He then declared the proceedings over.

The clerk repeated, "The court will rise" and Mr Justice Elderfield rose and left. Deborah was escorted into the judge's chambers for what reason Freddie had no idea nor was it anything to do with him. As he rose to leave the court he and the Group Captain met at the exit. This was the last thing Freddie wanted to happen and if looks could have killed he would have died there and then.

While waiting outside the courtroom the Group Captain came up to Freddie and remarked, "It's a sad and sorry day Fred but there you are." He gestured his hand for them both to shake and Freddie responded likewise. He was lost for words but, before he could say anything, the Group Captain continued saying, "It is ironic isn't it, I was the one who asked for a good reliable driver and you are that to me, and then you and my wife fall in love and as far as I'm concerned it is all over."

Freddie went to salute but just pulled back in time to convert his arm to a handshake. "Goodbye Fred, are you aware that you are standing to attention?"

"No sir, I must correct myself. It became a duty and a habit in your company."

"Well said Airman, well said," and Group Captain Churton left.

Deborah came out of the courtroom just in time to see the only two men in her life shaking hands. For the first time in this entire episode it gave her a shock, in herself she never thought it would have happened.

She broke down and cried clutching a bouquet of flowers. Freddie rushed to her as she was on the point of fainting. As in the past it cried, "Hold me, hold me Freddie."

A stranger came up to them saying, "There you've crushed your bunch of flowers." His action made them part and he continued, "The floor of this building has taken its fair share of tears over time and it will probably take some more in years to come," and then left. Who he was they were never to know.

They both left the court and headed for the first pub, hotel, café or restaurant, whichever came first. It was a pub that came first. They went into the saloon bar which was nicknamed 'The Divorced', The barmaid pre-empted their order. "Is it two brandies sir?"

"Yes, two large ones please, Miss." They had both been sitting down for what seemed like an endless time, but both could not bring themselves to talk. In reality, it was barely a moment.

Deborah broke this brief interlude by asking, "How did you come to be talking to Maurice?"

Freddie replied, "He came up to me and just said it was a sad day or something like that, and that he was the one who had asked Ft Lt Robertson for a quiet, reliable driver, and we both have ended up in court, though with nothing to say to it." It was not word for word but it would have to do. Deborah ordered another round of drinks. These too were doubles and, of course, they were getting tipsy. She confided to him that she felt a sense of freedom in finishing, then her voice became blurred and whatever else she was going to say, nothing left her lips and she fell asleep bolt upright. Freddie did not know what to do so he asked the landlord.

The landlord said to the barmaid, "We've got another one Ella. Put her in the back room." Then he looked at Freddie and enquired, "How about you, sir?"

"Oh I'm alright, thank you. If you don't mind I'll sit here and wait for her. It has been a great ordeal."

The time was approaching when the pub had to close and Ella went to wake Deborah. They both appeared from the room and Deborah said she was waking up anyway. Thanking the landlord and tipping Ella the barmaid, Freddie suggested they both catch a bus and get off at whichever London park came first, so they could take advantage of the lovely summer's day, be alone and talk things over. She kissed him and they left arm-in-arm. The park was St James', so they alighted and found a seat all to themselves.

CHAPTER 30

Freddie broke the silence which inadvertently they both had created by being in limbo. It seemed that neither knew what to say to each other so he gently eased the way by asking Deborah why the judge had wanted to see her in his chambers. At this point she remembered she had left the flowers at the pub. No matter. Freddie persisted. She said, "He wanted to offer his apology about doubting her word that her marriage had not been consummated. To him it was incredible, hence the bouquet of flowers."

Freddie then said to her, "We must have no secrets or mistrust between us when we are married."

Deborah perked up immediately saying, "Are you proposing to me, Freddie Radnor?"

"Yes, I am, Mrs Churton. I am."

"Well provisionally, until I am no longer Mrs Churton, I accept your proposal. Thank you, darling," sealing her reply with a kiss.

To make conversation he asked her how she had managed to get to Paris without any papers, seeing that her passport and identity card were at home.

"Why do you want to know dear?"

"No particular reason, only we are sitting here just watching the ducks."

"Oh alright then, here goes. I tried on two occasions but was thwarted by small events, but on that day when the bus taking us to the PX parked in the compound, it was third time lucky. When all the wives got off, I was the last one to leave but I stayed on. The driver checked that the bus was empty so I ducked down behind my seat. He then drove his bus outside the compound and parked it by the side of a big lorry. As I left the bus, two Yanks were talking and one said, 'Hey Chuck, where are you going?'

"'Paris. I'm all loaded up. I'm going to the diner to eat, then off to Headquarters just outside the city.'

"'You lucky son of a bitch.'

"I climbed into the lorry, laid down on some boxes and a half an hour later the driver moved off, unaware that I was in the back. I didn't care, Freddie, I didn't care. I was in such a state. I did have one scary moment at the Belgian border checkpoint. The driver was arguing with an official. The Yank started swearing and he told him 'Look you slimy, ungrateful bastards, until we leave Europe we're in charge'. There was some sort of a fight I think. I couldn't see. The Yank's final words to the officer were 'if it wasn't for us you'd still be under the Germans'. Then he got back into his cab and drove off as fast as he could. As a result I had quite a few bruises. When the Yank arrived at the HQ I picked my moment and ran and ran. I got onto the main road and hitched a lift to Paris. It's easy for a woman to do. The man dropped me at the railway station. He wanted you know what, Freddie. I said no at first but to get away from him I agreed to meet him later, but of course I had no intention of doing so. That is when I came across the nuns with the poor little orphans. You know the rest, dear. While I'm on the subject, at Maggadore I could have prostituted myself many times over, but I kept them all dangling on a promise. If I had given in to a certain senior officer I could have even got you a commission, but then I would have lost you."

Freddie attempted to stop her, but she over-ruled him saying, "Do you remember when Joan Elison and I were sick and you dried me as much as you could?"

"Yes I do, I will never forget that day. It was then I fell in love with you and that was the reason I took the necklace out of your handbag. I wanted to protect you. Doing what I did, drying you, meant below in my shorts, I was getting very excited. You know what I mean, don't you?"

"Yes, I felt you. I think had we been alone I would have had you there and then, when you were going all over my front you sexually excited me. You were the only man to caress me. But I suppose we have to thank Joan Elison in a way for stopping me from encouraging you to do it, thereby destroying my only weapon to end my marriage in an honourable way – failing to consummate it. Well dear it won't be long now. Just a little longer to wait. Tell me, Freddie, will it be your first time as well?"

"No. I became a man when you were in the same building."

"Do you mean the villa?"

"Yes."

"Who with?"

"The French air hostess in the room next to mine. Whoever suggested billeting her in there did me a favour. She came into where I was sleeping – if you remember there was a connecting inner door. Deborah, she handed it to me on a plate. She must have liked it a lot. I told her it was my first time and she told me in good English not to worry. She opened a bottle of champagne, the cork made a loud bang, then I heard steps and voices outside, was it you?"

"No, I heard it and sent Maurice to investigate as it sounded like a gun going off. So that was what it was! Maurice came back and tried to have intercourse with me. He must have known what was happening but I said 'no'. He knew the reason and I gave him the all clear to find it (sex) wherever he could. Did you ever drive him anywhere?"

"Did you like it?"

"At first for me it was over too quick, but she opened another bottle of champagne, gave me some more to relax me and it did the trick. The second time about two hours later, I was on top of her for some time."

"Are you going to do that to me?"

"I might," came his embarrassed reply. "Can we drop the subject Debbie, I'm beginning to feel frisky? Let's retrieve your flowers from the pub. It's nearly opening time." While on the bus he asked her how she came to have a French passport. She was now getting mildly annoyed by his inquisitiveness and told him to stop it and not to bring the subject up again.

"Please dear, wait until we're married and settled down, then we'll have plenty of time to talk." From Freddie there was silence, but at the same time he was bewildered: why not now? But she must have a reason.

Their bus stop was next so this ended all thoughts. The pub was still closed so Deborah said, "Oh I don't care, leave it. I don't want to carry the flowers about for the rest of the evening. It was too big anyway; it had attracted much attention for them both. They walked about for an hour or so then Deborah asked Freddie if he would mind if she went home, as she was not in the mood for anything. Freddie said, "No, of course not," and squeezed her hand. "You do what you want to." They said their goodbyes and parted once more.

CHAPTER 31

Finally the day of the Decree Absolute came and Deborah was free again. Her marriage and everything connected with it was now in the past. Even the love of her life was not with her, nor had she arranged to see him. In fact, two days before her agent had got her a cameo role in a film. It was her first venture into this industry. She had had a screen test and was told she was a natural. Whether this was true or the director was taken in by her looks and began to weave his way to get what most if not all men seek was uncertain.

Someone on the set whispered, "Be careful, he has got a reputation." She told Freddie and asked him for advice as she felt vulnerable. Freddie told her that if she wanted to do film work he would be on the set or even outside the studio. She would not be far away. Once more he was protecting her. A few days later he received a verbal message to go without delay to the Strand.

On arrival he was met by Richard who ushered him into the usual office to be told that they required him to undertake a courier mission to Paris. He was given scant detail, only the time and dates they provided. He enquired whether he had a choice. "No, you have not. If you refuse you will be in trouble. We are quite confident you are up to this work." He had to agree and in future was told not to question instructions, orders or anything else. He now realised what he had let himself in for.

Asking Richard what should he tell his parents or even, more important, Deborah, Richard told him it would be easier when they started him up in business, then no-one need know.

At this juncture in their talk Richard said, "Regarding Deborah why don't you take her with you? It would look better for us and you if you were travelling as a loving couple. This has been approved by the committee and it will be an all expenses paid trip."

Freddie was aghast at this suggestion but already he could see an advantage in all of this. Suddenly he became excited at the prospect. All he had to do now was ask Deborah if she would accompany him on his first foreign assignment. There was not much time – two days before he had to depart – but where was she? They had not arranged to see each other until the weekend. Many options came into his mind – send her a telegram, a letter, or go to her home? Putting these to Richard they were dismissed out of hand as he was not to tell anybody.

Then Richard came to the rescue, saying, "You're in London already, go to her agent." Of course, why hadn't he thought of that himself? 'Phoning Deborah's agent from Richard's office, they told him she would probably be at one of three theatres. All three were a few minutes away from each other. If not, there was no work and she would have gone home. Show business is like that. Enquiring at all three theatres, the answer was no. At one he was informed by the person he spoke to that, because of her manner they would not be employing her again. Asking why he was told to mind his own business and to please leave. So he had to resort to a telegram, writing 'D. Must see you today. Waterloo, 6pm. Freddie'.

All he could do now was hope she had returned home. It was early afternoon when he sent off the telegram so he went to the pictures to pass the time away. Eventually the time came round to go to Waterloo Station to await the train on which she would arrive at six. True to form he could see her waving to him above the heads of the other passengers. So close were these people walking they would not let her run towards him, but given half a chance she did and they embraced. Breaking off she asked what was the reason for the telegram and its urgency. He suggested they went into the station buffet where they could talk. Deborah quickly went to the counter and returned with two cups of tea. Freddie went straight to talk about the proposition from the Strand that she accompany him to Paris. She was shocked at first and sipping her tea remarked how expensive it would be for him. Telling her it would cost her nothing, she became suspicious of a catch. That was true. But all he was required to do was deliver a letter by hand and that if he was accompanied by a lady, meaning her, it would look good. And being a beautiful attractive woman, eyes would be on her and not on him.

"So it's dangerous?"

"No, this is a simple assignment. Oh come on, Debbie, how many girls get a chance like this?"

"What will my Mum and Dad think?"

"Deborah, you are over 21. I have just called you a girl because you are my girl. You can do whatever you want to do. I must have a yes or no. If you say no then they will find someone else."

The thought of this sealed it and she said, "Yes, I'll come with you. It's the chance of a lifetime." They both decided not to go anywhere that evening so she caught the next train home to tell her parents. What they would say did not bear thinking about! On parting, Freddie told her to stay at home and that somehow instructions by post would tell her what to do and he told her to carry them out to the letter. He said, "That is how I will get mine, or at the college."

After he kissed her he said, "I'm so glad you are coming with me." Little did both realise that the word 'coming' would change their lives. After seeing her on the train he went to the Strand to leave a message for Richard that Deborah had agreed to accompany him to Paris and both would carry out the instructions when they both received them. He then went to Paddington to catch his train home.

CHAPTER 32

They both received their instructions in the following day's post, unaware that both were slightly different in content, which alluded to when they arrived at Heston Aerodrome, particularly concerning when in the waiting room. The time that they had to be there and checked in by was by 10.30am on Flight H.12, departing at 11.00 hours. Deborah had arrived well before, in fact she had been there some time when Freddie came through the door. He made his way straight to her and immediately noticed that she had been crying. Her eyes were red where she had continuously been drying them. He asked her why and she told him that her father had all but thrown her out of the home, a place where she had many happy days as a child and through to adulthood, calling her a hussy and saying 'fancy going off to Paris with this young man'.

"Freddie I have brought everything I possess with me, but I cannot take all of it with me, but can only pack enough for five days, the length of our visit. Can I leave the rest here 'til we get back?" Freddie made enquiries for her. Some official said she could and that in any case the lady had too much for the flight. The same official then called out the passengers' names and seating numbers: "Mr F.W. Radnor and Mrs D.A. Churton." This completed they were all escorted to the aircraft which was a DC3. It brought back memories of India for them.

Deborah sensed what the love of her life was thinking, kissing him on his cheek she said above the noise of the engines, "It's you now, dear, not Maurice sitting beside me."

For the rest of the flight they just held hands until the plane touched down at Orly Aerodrome. The flight was uneventful except when after disembarking at Orly and they had been cleared at customs, Deborah assumed control of everything, the reason being she could speak the language. Suddenly in the arrival lounge an incident broke out. A man and a woman were running round trying to find their way out, being pursued by some burly men and the police. Also in the far corner of the lounge something else was going on. There was chaos everywhere. But somehow Deborah and Freddie escaped any attention, made an orderly departure and hailed a taxi to take them to their hotel.

The hotel was not the Ritz nor the King George but it was very imposing, at least from the outside. At the desk it came as a shock to them that a double room had been reserved in their real names. They looked at each other as if to say, was someone having a joke or was it part of the charade? Deborah asked in French whether there was a single room she could have and the answer was 'non'. Freddie had guessed that that would be the case and said to her, "Oh never mind, dear, we've done it before."

Deborah nodded in approval. They both signed in and were shown to Room 115. They unpacked, freshened up, then went out for a meal. That evening Freddie was not his usual self and in the hotel bar he was drinking whisky and sodas just as if he was drowning his sorrows.

Deborah could see what was happening and, stopping short of ordering him to stop having any more, she coaxed him to go up to their room. She succeeded and taking his arm walked him to the lift and into Room 115. She sat him down and she herself went down on her knees so she could look him in his face.

"What is the matter, dearest? Please tell me."

He said to her, "Do you remember that day when I drove you to one of your functions, just you and me and you had a lot to drink. You fell over, I picked you up and you asked me to bring some jewellery back to the UK. You had drunk a lot of whisky only because you needed some Dutch courage to ask me to do it."

"Yes, I remember, because you said no but changed your mind."

"Well," said Freddie, "Dutch courage is what I need tonight, so I am asking you, Deborah, simply will you marry me, here and now in Paris in the quickest time we can? Will you, as I cannot go on the way we are going."

Deborah herself broke down at this point and in amongst sobs said, "Yes I will. You have made me very happy. We will be alright together. First thing tomorrow we will find out how we go about it in France." Embracing him, utterly speechless, she got up and requested the hotel desk for assistance to get her future husband at least onto the bed, if only with his tie and collar undone. Her request was granted and she herself got undressed and got into the bed beside him and drifted off into a wonderful sleep. Awake first, she made sure he was alright. He seemed to be but was very pale, so she left him alone and got herself ready in the meantime, putting her personal items in her handbag and going down to the restaurant for something to take up to Freddie. It was suggested he had black coffee. She also while there asked for a directory of Paris. On returning to their room, Freddie had come round with a hangover. Sympathizing and comforting she told him to stay in until he felt better and poured him a cup of black coffee. She then told him she was going to the British Embassy as they were ordered to do in their letters and to find out who and where they both had to go to arrange their marriage.

Deborah had been gone about three hours when she returned, smiling and pleased with herself. "How are you, dear? Are you feeling better?"

"Yes much, much."

"Well I've had a great morning and I have found out a lot. First the MI5 man was pleased with what we did. Also that incident at the aerodrome, it was about two Russian Embassy staff defecting. One was very important, she was a cipher clerk and they got away. Next, yes, we can get married in three days' time, but we must both appear before the registrar together and show our papers. Also I managed to get a bank draft sent over from London so now my dear it won't be long. Does that cheer you up?"

"Yes it does. Soon we'll be together. But where are we going to live?"

"I've thought of that too. Months ago I came across a rundown terrace cottage in Maidenhead and I managed to get it quite cheap. I've done it up as best I could but it is our home, that's all that matters."

"Well I think you're wonderful, just wonderful," and he embraced her.

Losing no time they went to the registrar's office to register their intentions. Everything was in order. The time and date were fixed, but as usual there was a slight catch which was that until the wedding Deborah should stay at the Embassy for the next two nights because it would look better for all. Reluctantly Freddie had to agree. What was a couple of days now? Sitting in his hotel room alone, he began to ponder what had gone on in the past two years and came to the conclusion that had he not fallen for this beautiful woman he would have cleared off a long time ago. The thought of another man marrying, let alone taking away her virtue, soon dispelled his thoughts. Pouring another whisky there was a knock on the door and while making his way to open it he assumed it was a hotel porter, or even a mistake by someone knocking on the wrong room, which he judged must be the case. Unlocking the door, who should be standing there with red eyes was the woman who a few moments earlier had put doubts in his mind. Of course it was Deborah. The only thing she muttered was that usual phrase, "Hold me, Freddie, hold me." After a few seconds they broke away. He then asked her why she had left the Embassy and she said to him that it seemed to her that at every opportunity they (whoever 'they' are) were determined to keep them apart, even to the extent of stopping them getting wed.

"What makes you think that, dear?"

"Mr Jones or Lt Col. Hontas, whatever you want to call him, is at the Embassy now. He arrived yesterday and is making things difficult. Well I'm not putting up with it anymore, so here I am and I have called off our wedding on my own account. I hope you understand, Freddie. Once again I cannot take any more of people interfering in my life, let alone yours. So please pour me a whisky and I'll 'phone down to the desk to send up a bottle of champagne. Tonight is our wedding night. The ceremony can come later, back home."

The champagne duly arrived and the waiter did the necessary so proficiently as to be near perfect the way he did it. The waiter bid them farewell on leaving and Deborah in turn locked their door. "Well Freddie Radnor, let us toast to our life together, first with the whisky and then with champagne. They don't mix but who cares." Their glasses clinked. By now it was late evening and both were quite tipsy. Their inhibitions were slowly ebbing away. The look she was giving him said it all. She wanted him there and then. Freddie stood up and gestured for Deborah to do the same. Putting out her arms for him to help her, they were then face to face, both their hearts racing. Freddie led her to the bathroom. While still holding her he reached for a large bath towel, laid it on the floor and then another for her head to rest upon. She was by now undressing herself but before she could complete doing so poured some water down her front. It was a re-enactment of the time he had dried her off in India. "Caress me darling, caress me." She guided his hand down as he was re-enacting that same moment. Both by now on the floor, aroused to the height of passion, he entered her. She gave a yelp, a gasp. He in turn yelled:

"Deborah, Deborah. Deborah my love, we are now but one. You are wonderful. I love you so much."

She in turn, although breathless, said to him, "Thank you. You were so gentle and loving. You made it so easy for me. Now I feel a complete woman."

Freddie kissed her, and lifted her up together with the bath towel and helped her to bed. She did not want to lie down but sit up and requested a glass of champagne and a cigarette. The next thing they were both sitting up in bed sipping champagne and smoking. Life had never been so wonderful. Deborah asked him if he had in his case something she could put round her shoulders. Freddie gave her a choice of his pyjama top or a nice clean shirt. She opted for his shirt and he fetched it and put it around her. She buttoned it up with delight saying that's better. Sleeping with nothing on himself, they agreed to settle down for the night. All the champagne had been drunk, what lights were on were switched off and down into the bed they slipped.

As dawn was breaking she ran her hand over his body. Waking and aroused, he wanted no more persuading but to go with her again. This time it was different. The act took longer and was even more pleasurable and more comfortable in bed than on the bathroom floor. Both fell apart and returned to sleep, his arm around her waist as if to protect her. She was all the woman he imagined her to be, and she in turn thought the same thing about him.

CHAPTER 33

There was a tapping on their room door which awoke Deborah fully. She was in any case coming round from a beautiful sleep, feeling very fulfilled and above all a completely different woman. Rushing to find something to cover herself in she wrapped the large towel around her and went across to the door, calling out, "Who is it please?"

A female voice responded, "I'm from the British Embassy. I have your case and instructions for you." Opening the door just wide enough to take it and saying "thank you" to the messenger, also a waitress appeared with what the French call breakfast – coffee and croissants and a fruit conserve. Deborah said she was going to run a bath. Lapping up every moment, she was immersing herself. On coming out of the bathroom, now in a bath robe provided by the hotel, she said to her love, "You can have yours now, dear."

While Freddie was in the bath he heard her laughing and called out, "Why are you laughing, Deb?" She came in and told him that she realised she had not emptied the bath and that she had peed in it and began to apologise.

He stopped her and said, "Don't worry, I have as well." They both enjoyed the joke.

Later, Deborah asked him if he would mind her taking over the arrangements to leave for home as she could make herself understood in French. He replied,

"No, not at all. I'm only too pleased you can speak the language." By noon it was all done with. She had managed to get two seats on the 3.15 back to Heston.

Arriving back late that afternoon they went straight to Caxton Hall with ten minutes to spare before it closed and applied and got a special licence to be married. The registrar was satisfied with all their papers and told them the ceremony would take place at 11 o'clock the day after tomorrow, as there had to be one full day between applying and the ceremony itself. They both embraced, thanking the registrar as they left.

After leaving Caxton Hall Deborah went to the nearest 'phone box to make a call. While she was inside Freddie noticed that they were being followed. Up to this point he had been getting hungry but this unwelcome distraction took it away. When Deborah came out of the 'phone box he told her and she said, "Don't give it a second thought," and she told him she had 'phoned Mrs Noor and they had been invited to dinner that evening at Mrs Noor's apartment at 7 o'clock in Kensington. In the meantime they searched for somewhere for tea. Arriving at Mrs Noor's home, Deborah rang the bell and their hostess welcomed them both in.

After the two ladies kissed each other on their cheeks, Deborah introduced Freddie saying, "Your Highness, this is my future husband Frederick Radnor, who I am going to marry the day after tomorrow."

The Princess put out her hand and warmly shook Freddie's and said, "I'm very pleased to meet you, sir. I have heard so much about you. You are the gentleman I posted the registered letter for my true friend Deborah, to let you know where she was," and added, "When you are her husband, do look after her, she has been through so much, like myself but in a different way." He assured the Princess it was his only desire. Perhaps it was the wrong word but it did not matter.

A maid served cocktails prior to serving dinner, which turned out to be a wonderful experience for him. During the evening Deborah, asked Princess Devendra, if she would be a witness at the wedding.

"Yes of course," the Princess replied, thanking Deborah for the honour. About 10 o'clock, Freddie suddenly remarked while all three of them were drinking, smoking and chatting away:

"Darling, do you realise we have nowhere to spend the night?" At this Deborah gulped, saying she had forgotten. Devendra offered them the use of her guest room for not only that night but the next one as well. Also they could all leave for Caxton Hall in the same taxi. Freddie was so overcome by the Princess' hospitality that a small tear left his eye.

Before getting into bed they both sat talking. Among the topics was what to do about their parents. They came to an agreement that tomorrow they would part, each going to their respective homes and bring their personal belongings and tell their parents about getting married and that a reception would come later in the year. Also that while they were the guests of the Princess, no love making would take place. It appears that it is not the done thing. Neither was bothered. After breakfast Deborah told Devendra their plans. She understood and so the plan was carried out.

Freddie arrived back at the Princess' apartment first and they both sat talking in her small courtyard garden. It was here that the Princess broached the subject of a very valuable necklace made up of rubies, diamonds and pearls and asked him if he knew anything about it. He was shocked to the core but after a moment he regained his composure and told her that he had the necklace at his home. He assured her it was well hidden. The Princess' face became very stern.

Freddie did not know what to do. He was lost without Deborah, so he told Princess Devendra the story that when Mrs Churton and Mrs Elison were taken ill he removed it from Mrs Churton's handbag because if he had carried out his orders from Lt Col. Hontas, Deborah and possibly her Highness, would have been in serious trouble. Hontas has a reputation as a ruthless investigator. Your status would not matter to him. Deborah would have been linked to the safe robbery. That necklace would have opened the door and many people would have paid the ultimate price, prison. But as far as he was concerned, the case remains open. That is the truth. I only took it from her soiled handbag to protect her and nobody else. You see, I had already fallen in love with her and wished her no harm."

Freddie now had taken the whip hand and he and he alone was now in command of any situation. At this the Princess left her seat and embraced him, saying, "Thank you sir, so much." The embrace was seen by Deborah who had returned from her home.

"What is going on here?" Deborah demanded. The Princess rushed to Deb's side to assure her that it was a gesture of thanks for what her future husband had done for Deborah and herself, when against his orders from that nasty man Hontas he had taken from her handbag the necklace and in doing so saved both of them and probably more who were involved in what they were doing. At this she had to climb down and both walked over to Freddie, who at this moment in time was feeling rather pleased with himself. Two beautiful women vying for his attention – at least that is how it appeared to him.

That evening the threesome went out to dinner and a show in the Haymarket. They got back to the Princess' flat at around 11 o'clock and Deborah suggested they have a drink for no particular reason, but Devendra insisted on toasting it to Freddie.

"Alright," said Deborah, but to her Devendra appeared to be paying too much attention to and heaping praise on Freddie. Devendra sat next to him on a beautiful two-seater sofa. Also Devendra became the life and soul of the evening, even as she was pouring out the drinks, giving good measure to Deborah's glass and not so much to Freddie's. Then to Deb's surprise Devendra sat next to her on the even larger sofa and both began to giggle, all the time raising their glasses to their hero. All Freddie did was sit and enjoy himself. After all, it was his last night as a single man. It seems this was what all the giggling was about. They had cooked up something and it wasn't food, but what it was he didn't know.

But after a while Devendra went to the kitchen and brought in a bowl of snacks. While she was doing this Deb patted the sofa, indicating to Freddie to come and sit by her. He did not want asking twice to do so. When Devendra returned she, in turn, sat on the sofa. Now the saying, 'two's company, three's a crowd' came to Freddie's mind. But here he was sitting, and very close at that, in between two beautiful women. Who's complaining? he thought to himself.

All three retired to bed. During the night Freddie was woken by the Princess who told him that a noise had disturbed her, and not for the first time apparently. And it was true, there was evidence of an attempt to break in. He suggested she sleep with Deborah for the rest of the night and he would sleep in her bed. She thought it a good idea, but before they did Devendra got very close to him, so close it became an embrace and then a passionate kiss. As Freddie was still partially half asleep, he put up no resistance but broke away saying no in a most compassionate way. Devendra said:

"Yes, you're right, but perhaps one day we will." He kissed her on her cheek and she went to sleep with Deb. Devendra's bed was still warm. All the same, he was somewhat bewildered but drifted off. When he roused out of his sleep it was just past 8 o'clock, so he got up and made tea and coffee then took the tray to his two lady friends to rouse them. When Deb realised what had happened and who was beside her, she began shouting "What's gone on?" Devendra calmed her down by explaining what had happened in the night. Devendra seemed to have a hold over Deb. Both seemed very close as though they were two frightened sisters.

"How nice," Devendra said, "having tea in bed brought by a gentleman. You have a good husband Deborah."

"No, not yet, not until 11 o'clock. Then I will have and he will be all mine and mine alone."

CHAPTER 34

After breakfast all three went to their respective rooms to prepare for the ceremony. Freddie surprisingly came out last. He looked so handsome in his new suit, shirt and tie, all purchased from Harrods. In part he had used the £30 voucher Deb had given him prior to flying to West Germany. Deborah looked the part in a stunning two-piece suit and Devendra needed no compliments. The hired car arrived in good time. The driver loaded all their luggage into the boot and off they drove to Caxton Hall. In the waiting room prior to entering the hall where the ceremony would take place, Freddie introduced Debbie to his sister Mary, who in turn apologised for the absence of hers and Freddie's parents. Deborah put Mary at her ease saying her own were not present either, adding for good measure how parents can be very discerning.

The deputy registrar having checked who the couple were and in particular Deborah's divorce papers, ushered them into the marriage hall and the proceedings began at around 11.15 – they at last emerging into the sunlight as man and wife. The photographer put everyone in the place he wished them to be and last but not least the bride and groom alone. Deborah wanted to be photographed looking up at her new husband momentarily casting her mind back to their first meeting in India, cupping her hands around his to light up the cigarette he had offered her.

The happy couple drove off to the small buffet reception followed by Devendra and Mary, but as the car had some difficulty in getting into the traffic flow, Deborah caught sight of a tall handsome RAF Group Captain. It was of course the ex-husband Maurice – his single row of gold braid around the rim of his peak cap. In a flash their eyes met and being an officer and a gentleman he gave her a salute. A tear left her right-hand eye as it always did first when she was either happy or sad. The whole thing was over as soon as it began. For Mrs D. Radnor was now the happiest girl in the world.

As Deborah had no bridal dress to change into, it was easy to slip into the part of a well-dressed lady. The same applied to the groom – he just had to remove the carnation from his lapel and he was just an everyday man. As they left the reception, saying goodbye to everyone, Deborah was heard to say to Princess Noor:

"Well Devendra, it is now over between us. It is now really goodbye." Freddie heard this remark as he was in earshot and was puzzled by it. He asked Deborah in a quiet moment what the remark meant. Deb was caught off guard and brushed it off as nothing and she got out of it by taking Freddie's arm and strolling over to Princess Noor. On the way Deb said:

"As I have told you many times darling, when we are settled I promise you I will tell you everything." Changing the subject as they got towards the Princess, Deborah said:

"Devendra, Freddie and I would like to thank you for giving us the use of your house near Wentworth for our honeymoon." Even now there was a mystery.

"This is the first time I have heard about a honeymoon, why wasn't I told about this before?" He took her arm now and told his wife as diplomatically as he could that, "All this secrecy must stop from now on or your second marriage won't last long." Deborah had just seen a side of her husband she had not seen since that first night in Limoges. They said their goodbyes to everyone again and sped away down the A4 towards Wentworth.

CHAPTER 35

The house lay back off the main road and as their car drew up outside this very elegant house a maid appeared at the front door to welcome them. The driver took their luggage from the car's boot and Deborah tipped him a ten shilling note. Freddie thought, 'my goodness, that's a fair tip for a bit of driving'.

At this point Freddie drew a deep breath and started to draw on what he had heard in his relatively short life. Phrases such as 'start as you mean to go on', 'be self-assertive', and 'a few straight words are better than a lot of mixed-up ones over time', came to mind.

Once inside this imposing house he indicated to his new wife to come over to the French windows and stand beside him. Then he set to the challenge and asked her to come clean over everything and everyone that had passed in her life. He reminded her about the promise she made to him that she would do so once they were married.

Deborah was taken aback by his tone and attitude. She responded by asking him to pour her a glass of whisky. While he did, she opened her handbag for a cigarette. As a gesture she copied what she had seen in a film and lit up two and gave him one of them. Freddie also asked himself whether he had gone too far. It was too late now. Deborah broke the silence that had descended on them.

"Very well, you are right, let's get it over and done with." She rang for the maid who came very quickly.

"Yes Madam, what can I do for you?" Deborah requested that they did not wish to be disturbed under any circumstances.

"I will ring for you later."

"Yes Madam, I understand."

"Well sweetheart, fire away."

"Why did you not tell me where we were going to spend our honeymoon?" asked Freddie.

"Because you never asked, dear."

"I assumed we would go to your house in Maidenhead."

"How on earth do you know I have a house in Maidenhead and who told you? That house is my wedding present to you. Also it is not my house any more, it is ours. But how did you find out? As far as I'm aware only my solicitor, the agent and my bank knew of it," Deborah replied.

"Well a few months ago I was summoned to go to the Strand, what for I had no idea. Richard the link man told me nothing was wrong, only they [MI5] wanted to ask me some questions. When I was ushered into a room there were three senior officers. A few moments later Lt Col. Hontas came in and he took over."

Freddie then told Deborah that they asked him about her buying a house in Maidenhead.

"What a bloody cheek," Deborah retorted.

"Yes. That is more or less what I told them and I reminded them that Mrs D. Churton's business was her own and that it was none of mine and it was none of theirs. I got out of my chair and walked out. Richard asked me to stay on while I filled in an expenses form.

Deborah, what they gave me was quite a lot of money, probably to say nothing to nobody. So there you have it, Deb, that is how I knew that you had bought a house. I thought it best to say and do nothing. I don't know where the house is or what plans you have, but as we are now married and you kept me waiting until we were, here we are as one."

Deborah got closer to him and held his hand. The situation had changed. She now knew she had married the right man. He in turn drew her close and held her in his arms. Their eyes met and they kissed as newlyweds should.

"OK sweetheart, what's the question, as if I didn't know. It's about my relationship or friendship with Princess Devendra, am I right?"

"Yes, to me you both seem very close," Freddie replied.

"Yes, we are. But what we both set out to do has been successful, so our friendship will be less intense. You, dear, will take her place. I met her at a big house party given by her brother. Everyone who was anyone was invited. Her brother, a rich prince, was obsessed with me, so much so he wanted me to divorce Maurice and marry him. I had to tell him the English do not do that sort of thing. But he would not take no for an answer. But of course he had to. I had to threaten him by informing the district officer. Then out of the blue, through his father, it was suggested a few wives of service officers should be invited to their father's retreat in the highlands during the hot season. The British called them hill stations. Of course it was a ruse to get me away. Maurice was all for it. I think he was hoping I would return a more congenial wife. Only a few from RAF Maggadore were invited. Joan Ellison was not among them. Up until that point we were good friends.

"Princess Devendra was appointed my chaperone and that is how we became good friends.

"You see, dear, the top and bottom of the whole set up was all the princes, their palaces and money, jewellery, would be confiscated when India became independent. They had heard of what happened to the Russian royal family and their cronies so they had to get everything of value that they had out of the country and as they knew England and the English that is where they had to send it, any way they could.

"Freddie darling, it was organised like a military operation. There had to be someone in India to get it out, hence ordinary ranks were used, as they would not be under suspicion as they would have no money to buy anything, let alone smuggle valuable items and cash. Joan Ellison was good at it. I tried but was useless. That is why four of the drivers Maurice had requested had to return to normal duties. You were the seventh, but you revealed to me in your way you were not going to do it or have any part, so when I fell in love with you, I was determined to keep you out of it. No-one knew about it until some bloody fool robbed the station safe. It is still a mystery about who did it. Enter Mr Jones, alias Lt Col. Hontas, which put an end to the operation. Everybody from RAF Maggadore arriving back in the UK was searched, but they still found nothing."

At this point Freddie put his hand over Deb's mouth, stopping her from saying any more and quietly gestured that they would go outside into the garden. Somewhat puzzled at this, Deb opened the French doors and both walked into the garden. He then asked her to go into the maid's quarters and start to strike up some sort of friendship, try and get to know her, get her confidence.

"Why, why, why, dear?"

In short, "Walls have ears." Deborah grasped the situation at once and strolled off on some pretext to the maid's quarters. Freddie came back inside and looked around but could see no obvious signs of any disturbance and thought to himself perhaps he was over-reacting. But at the same time thought 'you never know!'

Deborah was gone some time – about forty minutes. When she came back she looked radiant and very happy with herself, telling him she was sorry but as they both got talking they had a lot in common. She told Freddie that she was not a maid but a housekeeper. Her parents, like you and I, were brought up and lived in a council house and like me wanted to be in show business, but things turned out different for her. "Come Freddie, and meet her. Her name is Jane. Also she has a meal for us and I insisted that we sit in the kitchen, including herself. Come along, dear, and meet her as an equal. It's much better." And it was.

CHAPTER 36

Although it was by now late August, that evening it began to get dark and a thunderstorm developed. There was not much to do and Deborah was immediately taken back to India and the monsoon season and suggested to Freddie that they should invite Jane to make a threesome. Jane was delighted to join in and a pleasant evening was had. All three got on well. Pennies were played for and Jane won. They all had a nightcap and retired to bed. Deborah and Freddie did not want to go to sleep just for a while so they both talked about the future after their brief honeymoon was over.

They undressed, got into bed and held each other. Deborah began, "I think we should go to Maidenhead tomorrow and I'll show you our house, for that is where our future begins. We are a lucky couple, dear. Not many these days can do that." He held her closer and more firmly, kissing her passionately. Putting out the bedside lights and in the stillness of the night, murmurs of pleasure drifted from their bed. Afterwards they were both out of breath and had difficulty saying "night night" to each other.

The second day of their honeymoon was a Saturday and after breakfast they set off by train and bus to where their cottage was situated. Arriving at No. 7 Teddington Terrace, Freddie was pleased to see it was an end property and told Deborah so. She opened the front door and went to go inside but Freddie stopped her.

"Why did you do that, dear?" He grabbed her and lifted her up in his arms. "To carry you over the threshold, my love." And he did, but soon had to put her down as she was quite heavy. They embraced and kissed. They had arrived at the destination both had been seeking.

The first thing Deborah did was apologise to him saying, "I'm sorry, sweetheart, it's not much but it's a start." Freddie gasped and lightly rebuked her for even thinking such a thing.

"Many couples in 1949 have no place at all. I am very lucky! Both of us are. We have our own front door key."

At that Deb pointed to a small box on the sideboard saying, "What's inside is yours, my sweet. Open it and see."

"Really, all right," and he did. Inside were two pairs of keys, one for the front door and the other set for the back. He was overcome by his emotions, which he had always been able to control in the past. After all of this she showed him around their home. It needed quite a lot of renovation but was nonetheless habitable. It was just as it had been built in late Victorian England with a brick floor and a brick copper for boiling clothes. No bathroom, two bedrooms and a small box room over the top of the scullery.

To Freddie it was just one better than that hovel in Limoges, but he kept his thoughts to himself and thinking about Devendra's two homes and particularly the one at Wentworth, it was 'after the Lord Mayor's Show followed the dust cart'. He was grateful to her and told her so. What there was in the way of furnishing was functional and that's all. Lighting up cigarette after cigarette he could not leave for Devendra's house in Wentworth quickly enough.

Deb suggested they went into Maidenhead for something to eat and drink and they found the café where back in March they had said their goodbyes before Deb left for West Germany. But as a consolation he could say that that was not the situation now. This lifted his spirits and brought him back to reality.

Over their meal Deborah began to reflect back to that most unhappy day. She told him that when she left him to catch her train she sobbed all the way to the station and that when she got to the platform almost at the same time the train pulled in and the porter said "hello" and he opened the carriage door for her.

"I got in but without him seeing me I got out and hid in the ladies' waiting room. Then I saw you walk over the footbridge to your platform. I followed you and hid behind a large pillar and watched you. You turned around quickly but I managed to duck down."

"Freddie interrupted her at this point saying, "I did sense that I was being followed. So it was you." Holding her hand across the table, "What did you plan to do?"

"I nearly called out to you, don't go Freddie, don't go, but your train came and you were gone."

"Dear, what would you have done if you had called out to me?"

"I don't know. I was in a state of confusion." He then told her about picking up the paper on the seat and staring him in the face was Ginger Towner, the safe breaker who was at Maggadore and who had confessed to the station safe robbery, thereby solving the mystery. Deb on hearing this nearly choked over her food, so astonished was she.

"So there it was meant to be, you did not call out and stop me from going home. Tell me Deb, if you had called out, where would we have gone?"

"Well that's typical of me not thinking! I have doubts now about our house. You're right, Freddie, it's not for us, it's just an empty cold place still in wicked Victorian England. They were so cruel to the working poor. In future Freddie we will do things and make decisions together. I'm no good by myself." They left the café arm-in-arm to walk to the station to go back to Devendra's lovely house in Wentworth for a life of luxury for the next two days.

On the journey back to Devendra's house both were very quiet, holding hands. It was obvious they were thinking what to do next. Freddie made a suggestion to her that he had come to the simple conclusion that wherever they lived, other than the cottage, they would have to pay rent, which was no problem as both had work and a decent living. He was working for the Strand and she had her bit parts in show business. He suggested that they both approach Devendra to see whether she could help until their cottage was ready to live in. Deb thought it a good idea and they both decided it was worth a try.

On returning to Wentworth they tried in vain to get through to Devendra's London home, so all they could do was resume what was left of their honeymoon until Monday, when they would begin their life together. When they awoke on the Sunday, Deb surprised Freddie by saying she wanted to attend morning service at the local church alone and asked if he would mind. "No of course not. You do what you want. I'll stay here and try to contact Devendra."

CHAPTER 37

It was a lovely autumn day and in the afternoon they decided to go and have a second look at the cottage as the state of the place was such a shock to him that he failed to see its potential. It was like keeping looking in a shop window. You went away but kept going back to have a second or even a third look before going in and buying whatever it was!

While Debbie attended morning service, Freddie tried to contact Devendra. He was not successful and was getting slightly frustrated so he went to Jane's quarters to see if she had any means of contacting her mistress as he could not. Jane told him that it would be impossible before midday as Devendra took sleeping tablets, as well as retiring to bed very late and she suggested he try after that time. He told Debbie what Jane had said and also asked her how her church service had gone. She replied that it went very well and she had left the service totally refreshed.

Deborah 'phoned after lunch and got through to a drowsy Devendra and told her of their predicament and asked if she could help. "Yes of course, but I had better come down this afternoon to show you the rooms and terms of your stay. I will arrive around tea time."

Debbie informed both Jane and Freddie. All three were excited about the prospect of them being able to stay, most of all Jane as she got very lonely at Wentworth in such a large house. Her 'Highness', as Jane had to address her, came in her personal car alone – in fact it was not her car at all, it was a pre-war sports which her brother used to go to rallies in. He was a playboy and well known in social circles. Jane had to greet her at the main entrance. Deb and Freddie watched from a side window, amazed to see how Jane greeted her mistress.

Freddie looked Deb in the face and said, "What are we in for now?" Freddie should not have worried as Devendra warmly embraced both of them and the attention was one of friendship and understanding. They came to an arrangement which suited both parties, i.e. they could for a nominal rent have two rooms which would in the pre-war days have been additional servants' quarters, after Monday, when their honeymoon would be over. Debbie suggested that Jane should come in and be told what was going to happen. Devendra reluctantly agreed and Jane was summoned in. Again Devendra surprised Freddie when she said, "Let's all have a drink on that." It was a trait Freddie had noticed before – her Highness' mood would, together with other situations, change in a flash. Devendra then got out of her chair and showed them what rooms would be theirs. Debbie and Devendra again embraced and Devendra bid them farewell, racing off in her brother's sports car.

The threesome, to put it mildly, were amazed. The drinks were never poured. Why Devendra had suddenly left was anybody's guess, so Debbie said, "Never mind. Now all three of us are equal, let's go to the pub this evening and have one there." But Jane told them she was not allowed to leave the house unattended – it was a condition of her employment. So for the time being it was left at that. The happy honeymooning newlyweds went by themselves. After all, it was their last night as Devendra's guests.

The next morning Jane knocked on the newlyweds' door, placing the tea tray on the small table outside. Freddie collected it and poured them both a welcome cup. Sitting upright and savouring her cup, Debbie said, "Well darling, from today we set off on our journey into everyday married life. How do you feel?"

Freddie replied, "Wonderful. We have had to go through much trauma to get here."

Deborah put down her cup, leaned over and kissed him. In the kitchen all three had breakfast and afterwards Deb went upstairs to move out of the master bedroom into the servants' quarters, telling Jane what she had done and that the room was now vacant. "We are all equal now, Jane. You can go out in the evenings when we are here. Who knows, you may meet a nice young man and settle down."

"But what about the Princess?"

"Oh, don't worry about her, I can handle Devendra." At this remark Freddie took a mental note! Also he told Debbie that he had made out a list of what they had to do and showed it to her. She was shocked by it and read it to herself three times. The last two items concerned both their respective families. At this Deb baulked and said no, inventing any excuse she could think of. But Freddie told her, "It's best to get it over with," ending by telling her he had noticed there was a garage about a mile away where he could hire a car. If he could get one everything on the list could be completed.

At the thought of this Debbie caved in and told her new husband, "Dearest, once more you are right." The most important thing was to make their cottage their home, despite whatever the condition it was in. It would be their base for everything. The post, bolt hole, come what may. They left the family visits until last, as in the evenings they would be home from work. They need not have worried as it all went well. Debbie's father had mellowed, which added to her happiness.

When they returned to Wentworth, Deborah fancied a large whisky but there wasn't any. Her life in particular had come full circle. She was now back to where she had started, just a working-class girl, albeit a married one. Freddie had never left it and he, not for the first time, came to her rescue. He said he would buy her a half bottle while he returned the car to the garage. She even said to him, "That's a good idea." No darling or sweetheart, but just "don't be too long." Jane looked at Freddie with a disapproving look but said nothing. She knew she had to keep her own counsel. Freddie also picked this up. He thought it better to buy a half bottle just to see how long it would last. He already knew by her letters from West Germany, also in India, that her drink was whisky. She thanked him and her mood changed.

CHAPTER 38

The following day Freddie 'phoned Richard to tell him where he and his wife were staying, but he was not available. His secretary took all the details and said she would pass them on. Later in the day Richard returned his call and told him to 'phone from a public call box and not to 'phone from Wentworth again. Deborah got work straight away. She had a walk-on part in a play in the West End, so he met her every night at the station and walking home arm in arm neither of them could be happier. Freddie was somewhat puzzled by Richard's insistence only to 'phone from a public call box. The next day he was told to resume the course at the technical college and await further instructions. If he did that they would know where he was.

In hiring a car, Freddie thought back to his days in the RAF and how convenient cars were! He had forgotten that Mr Brown had bid for the Humber Snipe at the auction and so he made up his mind to get it roadworthy. In the rush to get married he had neglected one or two people and Mr Brown was one. So one day he skipped the college to see him and try to get the car going. He was sure the reason nobody could start it was the isolation switch under the dashboard. He did a spot check for oil and petrol and there seemed to be enough to try. He put his left hand under where the switch was, pulled the starter and she fired first time. Mr Brown was amazed. There and then Freddie decided to find a small garage and have it looked over. After eyeing around and vetting any garage that came his way he chose one that suited his instinctive intuition! It was run by two recently-demobbed blokes who had set up in business, one was an ex-RAF flight engineer. They even offered to go to Mr Brown's yard and tow the car to their garage, so Freddie gave them the job.

Returning to the tech. college, he was handed a letter. He knew who it was from – the Strand. Its contents both surprised and shocked him. It requested that he come to the address above, accompanied by his wife, to be interviewed on Wednesday the 4th of October, which was the following week. When he showed it to Deb, she too was surprised and reached for a whisky and a cigarette. She was worried why? If she had known there and then, she would have not had either! Freddie took it in his stride. In the meantime nobody had heard anything from Devendra – not even Jane, whose wages were paid by money order through an agency which told them nothing.

They did not have to go to the Strand but the house in West London where Freddie had been before. They were met by Richard who, when he saw Deborah, was taken aback by her attractiveness and beauty. He quickly offered them refreshments. Soon after both were ushered into a large room where the three usual men were sitting behind a desk. Freddie had met them before so Deborah was introduced to all three. They too were taken aback by her looks.

She was immediately put at ease by being told that she had no need to worry. She had done nothing wrong.

Freddie took a back seat. It did not bother him. But within a few moments both were shocked to the core when Col. Hontas suddenly appeared through another door. Deborah immediately leapt from her chair and in a loud voice said, "What is going on here?"

She became flushed with rage. Col Hontas responded, "Please calm down, Mrs Radnor, all I want to do is to ask you how and why you befriended Princess Devendra and her family, and how you managed to get thousands of pounds worth of jewellery and money from India to the UK, and where is it kept? You see, in a week's time I retire and I would like to know the truth. You can rest assured you, nor anybody with you, are in any trouble, and I will be able to retire with the satisfaction of solving every case and investigation I have dealt with."

Deborah looked around the room and then she looked every person in the face, above all her Freddie. He nodded and said, "Yes, get it out of everybody's way and be done with it."

Deb said, "Very well, but can I have a glass of whisky and a cigarette, please?"

Four of the men present nearly fell over themselves to grant her wish, they were so enthralled by her beauty and attractiveness. Her wish was over-subscribed – three whiskies too many! Deborah began by reminding everyone in the room that India would get its independence from Britain sooner rather than later and that two years on, when the day came, no-one knew what would happen. Those people in high positions from the Maharajahs, Sultans, the rich, and those of a higher caste were convinced that there would be much bloodshed – in fact a revolution not seen since the Russian one in 1917.

"So everyone wanted to get their valuables and money out of India and they came to the conclusion that the best place was England. But how to get it there without paying duty on it was a big question. The answer came from an army intelligence officer who got the idea from the resistance movement in Europe where he had been sent to operate. The solution he came up with worked better than some of the plans in the war. It was so simple it would not be discovered until it was too late. Being an intelligence officer he went through the service records and selected his recruits, particularly those returning home to be demobbed. If they agreed they would be given a post-dated cheque. On arrival in the UK they would be met and in secret all the contents in their kit bags, which was not theirs, would be handed over to the contact. Then cash would be exchanged for the return of the cheque. Then it would be taken and placed in safe deposit boxes in London. Each item was carefully recorded as to whom it belonged to.

"Bank accounts were opened in false names and money was transferred by banks in India to the banks in the UK. It all went like clockwork, but right at the end some bloody fool robbed the safe at RAF Maggadore, which brought you to the station where my then husband Wing Commander Churton was second in command and you, Colonel Hontas, linked the two together. But they were miles apart. As you got nowhere with your investigation you asked for another driver for my then husband, who would drive us around to see if he could do your work as an undercover airman. Am I right Colonel?"

"Yes, so far you are."

"The Airman you or Flight Lt Robertson chose was a very different driver from the others. He stood out a mile and it went round the officers' mess to beware and everyone buttoned up. That is why he heard and saw nothing. What he did not see or hear he could not tell you. Yes I did ask him, but he said no. He should have reported that to you, but unaware to me at the time he had fallen in love with me, the Wing Commander's wife, and could not bear to see me get into trouble.

"It was shortly after Mrs Elison and myself were taken ill that I realised I had fallen in love with him. The rest you know. Now Colonel, is that all?"

The Colonel replied, "Yes, that is all I want to hear." He got out of his chair, came round the desk and shook her hand and said, "How strange life can be. One by one I had you all lined up. One by one, from the Princess down to everyone, including the CO, your first husband and everybody on the station. But thanks to your present husband and his vigilance on reading a simple everyday newspaper, I have all the answers I require to close the case which I now will do." Deborah already knew what Freddie had done by removing the necklace from her handbag when she was taken ill with Joan Elison. He had also told her about Ginger Towner.

The Colonel shook hands with all present and bid them farewell. Deborah asked, "Is that why my husband and I were invited to this meeting?"

"No," answered the same man in the centre of the three, the same one who had interviewed Freddie.

By now it was lunch time but before the proceedings came to a conclusion the same man who was in the centre asked if they would all leave for lunch, everyone except Mrs Radnor. Everyone was mildly surprised. Freddie even asked the reason but he was rebuked. All present then got out of their seats and filed out, even the two secretaries. Deborah was left by herself with the three men.

Outside, Freddie was annoyed and went down to the canteen with Richard. But after taking four steps he stopped and asked Richard if he would stay and escort his wife to the canteen where he would be. Richard said he would be honoured and proud to do so. Jokingly he said, "I would like to take your wife anywhere." Freddie took this as a compliment and continued down the stairs. As he queued in the unit's canteen he could not let Colonel Hontas sit by himself and after paying at the till sat down opposite the Colonel.

"Do you mind, sir?" he enquired.

"No, not at all. I expect you're wondering why your wife was asked to stay behind. Let me put you at ease. Let's just say they want to talk to her in confidence. She will be here in a moment." Freddie immediately picked up a side of Colonel Hontas he had never seen before. He had mellowed or he was content that any loose ends had been tied up. The Colonel then gave Freddie another shock by mentioning that his wife was pleased she would be able to see more of him and they would be able to spend more time at home and take up their joint passion for golf.

"You surprise me, sir, you have never mentioned your wife before."

"Why should I young man, this is the first time we have met informally." At this remark Freddie had shown his weak side.

The Colonel and Freddie were involved in a serious conversation when the Colonel came out with an astonishing remark, telling Freddie that had he chosen to stay in the RAF he would have recommended him for a Commission, on account of his appearance and attentiveness. Freddie thanked him for that and said, "Strange that, sir. You're the second person to have told me that. If nothing else it is nice to know."

With that the other person to do so came into the canteen. It was of course Deborah with Richard, who came over to where Freddie and the Colonel were sitting and said, "Here you are Fred. I reluctantly hand your beautiful wife back to you."

With that the Colonel got up, shook everyone's hands and for the second time said, "Goodbye." Deborah was so excited she was finding it difficult to eat her dinner, but Freddie quietly told her to eat it and tell him outside. He also noted she had a large buff envelope, too large to go into her handbag. Freddie told her to hide it any way she could.

"Why, dear, why?"

"Never mind, I'll tell you later as I know what is in it." So she just managed to put it in her handbag folded. To get him back to the man he was most of the time she had known him, Deborah remarked how delicious her dinner was and said she would love to eat here every day. This brought Freddie to his old self so the remark had worked and she finished her meal in a relaxed mood.

CHAPTER 39

When they got back to Wentworth they found Jane in a desolate state, her eyes were red where the tears had been flowing like a waterfall. Deborah instinctively rushed to her side to comfort her and looked at Freddie to make himself absent – this was no time for any man to be around. About an hour later Deborah called Freddie to come in and put him in the picture as to Jane's reason for crying. "It appears it is over her son. In short, dear, Jane cannot have him here because Devendra will not allow it and she has had a letter from her parents telling her that if she does not come and collect him he will have to be put to be fostered. I have managed to calm her down so do you have any suggestions, dear?"

"Yes, a simple one. Let's 'phone for a taxi and the three of us go to wherever her parents live and bring the child here and sod Devendra."

Deborah went straight into his arms, crying, "Dearest, you have said what I wanted you to say. Bless you, bless you." She broke away to run to tell Jane, whose response was one of great relief. Freddie came into Jane's room and said that the taxi would arrive in about five minutes and he asked Jane if she had the baby's birth certificate.

Jane said, "Yes, but why?"

He then drew Deborah aside and told her, "If there is any confrontation, bring this up," also telling her to stay in the taxi unless Jane ran into trouble, and he would stay there to look after the house.

The taxi arrived and off they went, hoping it was not too late and that the child was still at her parents' home. Freddie had made other plans if Jane's baby had been taken away into care. While he was waiting for a 'phone call or for them to return he wondered what the little boy's name was and to pass the time wrote some names down on a piece of paper. Some were quite outrageous, some names from film stars. Winston was first and he smiled to himself as it was too obvious.

That was as far as he got when he heard a car door slam. They were back. He rushed out to greet them. They had been gone about half an hour and there seated in the back was Deborah nursing the baby. Her first words to him were, "Freddie, dear, pay the driver would you as you see I have my arms full with this bundle of joy." She then passed him to Jane, whose face even in the dim light of the porch was a sight to behold.

The child was fast asleep as if it knew what was happening – he was with his natural mother. At this point Freddie asked Jane what his name was. Before she could answer Deborah said, "It's Andrew." But Freddie rebuffed her, stating:

"I asked Jane, not you dear." Deborah left and went to their quarters. Jane looked up and asked him if he would leave as she wished to feed him. He suddenly realised what Jane meant – she did not want to expose her full breasts which were large and full of nourishment for her baby. This was a part of life Freddie knew nothing about.

It was good timing. As he followed Deborah's footsteps up to their rooms, Deb was upset at being rebuked and without asking poured them both what was left of the half bottle of whisky but neither of them could take the first sip. She did what she always did in these situations.

"Hold me, Freddie, hold me." Afterwards all was well. Then completely changing the subject he asked her what had happened when she was asked to stay behind, as if he did not know. She told him that she had been invited to join MI5. The reason was that they had been impressed by her resourcefulness when she left the RAF station and her husband. Also they had spoken to a doctor about why she did it, who had said in simple terms she was on the verge of a nervous breakdown. The doctor said he was sure she was a classic example, that in nine cases out of ten running away from everything for a while solves all what is troubling them, but some come back and it starts all over again. Freddie told her to read it carefully, think about it and make up her own mind.

"That is what I did. It was on the recommendation of Colonel Hontas." Deborah got halfway through reading the document, undressed ready for bed and invited Freddie to do the same, where they could talk more comfortably – the chairs in the servants' quarters were not very comfortable. Both were sat up and Freddie said he was running out of money.

Deb said, "So am I but tomorrow I'll go to London and get some from my bank." This was the first time he had heard that she even had a bank account. He himself said he would go to the cottage in Maidenhead to collect the mail; the Strand might have sent his money orders there.

Deborah then completely changed the subject when she came out with what could only be described as a bombshell. It was that she was yearning for a child of her own and the sooner the better. She asked Freddie why she had not conceived as he had never taken precautions. He did not know what to say.

"Well if you like we'll try tonight, but that's all we can do." She invited him to do his best. He did not refuse or make excuses. She felt his warm love come into her, hoping it was a full moon or something. It might do the trick! Only time would tell.

The following morning Deborah was in high spirits. She told the love of her life what she was going to do that day. She would go to London to get some money and 'phone Devendra to tell her what had happened at Wentworth regarding Jane having her baby returned to her. After all it was only natural and right and at the same time in Deborah's mind, keeping her thoughts to herself, if anybody knew Devendra it was her. Today their friendship welded in India would be put to the test. Both decided over breakfast where they would be going.

Then the 'phone rang. It was for Freddie from the Strand, telling him not to shave or have a haircut for three days and then to report to the house in West London when the three days were over. If anyone asked to just say it is was medical thing, but if possible stay in out of sight and that was an order and wait for further instructions. Freddie confided all of this to Deborah before she departed for London to see Devendra over Jane and her baby.

The two left behind at Wentworth, Jane and Freddie, were wondering how things would turn out. As the gardener had not for one reason or another come in to work, Freddie took it upon himself to do whatever he thought needed to be done and if Devendra were to be difficult it might be a sop to sweeten her up. In the afternoon Jane called out to him that he was wanted on the 'phone. She said, "It's your wife."

All Deborah said was, "Darling, please meet me at Weybridge Station in half an hour."

Of course he said, "Yes." Jane asked if there was a decision and he replied, "I don't know, Jane, but we will soon find out."

The train had hardly come to a halt when the first carriage door opened and who should alight, none other than Deb. She ran towards him as fast as her legs would take her and straight into his arms, muttering in between sobbing, "Take me home, Freddie, take me home. I wish the pub was open then I could have a drink."

"Whatever happened for you to be in a state like this?"

"Just get me home, please, then I'll tell you!"

Arriving at Wentworth Deb went up to their rooms. Freddie took it upon himself to raid Devendra's drinks cabinet and poured her a whisky. By now he knew how she liked it – ice and soda. Deb began by saying, "When I got to her apartment in Kensington her maid said she was still asleep, so I went to the bank, got some money and came back. By then she was up, but only dressed in a slip. I then told her what had happened about Jane and her baby. Freddie, dear, she exploded and we had a ferocious row. I finished up telling her she was not a princess in India now but a guest in England and that our friendship was at an end, then I stormed out. Freddie dearest, she was still in her nightdress and a silk wrap and she chased me in the street. When she caught me she begged me to come back and talk things over. I had no choice, everybody was looking, if only for her sake.

"When I agreed she kissed me and we walked back to her apartment arm-in-arm. When we were back inside the first thing she did was to call in the maid and cleaner and gave them two pound notes each and told them to go out and treat themselves – just like my parents did for me, particularly on a Sunday afternoon. They did not want telling twice. When they had gone, Devi calmed down. We both had a glass of whisky and a cigarette. She then asked me to run her a bath. In no time at all she was back to her normal self. We went out to lunch then went back to her apartment until I left to catch the train home."

Freddie said, "Deb, stop there. I don't want to hear any more, please."

"Why did you say that to me?"

His reply was, "You two seem very close to me, too close."

Deb said, "Yes, we are, it is because of what happened to us in India and I suppose you want another explanation? The last time you raised your voice to me was in Limoges. Sometimes I wish I was still there, but the thought of you made me decide to contact you again.

"Freddie, we've only been married a month and I sense some friction creeping in. Please don't let it happen, after all look that we've been through to get where we are."

He was quick to realise she was right and now he went to her and said, "Hold me Deb. I'm sorry. I'm a bit on edge as tomorrow I go solo on my first assignment. I don't think it is very important but all the same..."

There she stopped him, saying, "I'm sure you will be OK. They must think you're up to the work they will be giving you; otherwise you wouldn't have been taken on. Besides, the wages are good, so good in fact I have decided to fill in this form and join myself, if they will have me." On hearing this he was overjoyed and he too poured himself a glass of whisky, and clinked glasses with the love of his life, his wife and friend. All was well, but at the same time she did not like his unshaven face, hoping it was not for a week or more.

CHAPTER 40

Freddie's instructions came with the evening post and were as follows:
'Make your way to Weybridge Station at 07.30 hours. There you will be approached by a man from a council and taken to their highways department and given some overalls. You will sweep a long road until you get to number 43. Leave your hand truck outside and knock on the door of 43 and ask whoever answers if you could possibly use their lavatory as it is urgent as there are no public ones nearby. If the person agrees, go to where it is and see if you notice anything, anything unusual. If they offer you anything, do not refuse. Always take a mental note of what you see. Then make out a report for us to study. Then carry on sweeping until you are picked up some hours later. You must use your own initiative. Then let us have your report delivered by your hand the day after. Signed R.'

All three of them were in Jane's kitchen having breakfast. Both Deb and Jane remarked light-heartedly that a beard did not suit him. Freddie himself agreed but he had no choice as he was under orders as he was in the RAF and he was more concerned about shaving it off than the task given to him.

As he left Deb had already had baby Andrew in her arms. She looked radiant. It was, he thought, what she wanted more than anything else – a child of her own. This mildly played on his mind on his way to the station but he had his first real assignment which had to take priority. He was duly picked up and driven to the depot where he was given his trolley, brooms and shovel and started to work his way along several streets and roads, so that by 10.30 he would be sweeping the road outside the house in which he had to request the occupant the use of their lavatory. Here a touch of nervousness took over, but he had to go through with it. Freddie rang the door bell and a rather attractive lady opened the door.

"Yes, what is it you want? You're the road sweeper aren't you?"

"Yes, madam, I am and could I possibly use your toilet please as I don't know what to do."

"Yes of course, it is at the top of the stairs, first door on the left."

"Thank you lady, you're most kind." In fact he did use it. He flushed the bowl and came down the stairs. There the lady was, waiting to show him out, but instead of doing so she asked him if he would like a cup of tea.

"Oh yes, please, I would." And she invited him into the kitchen and indicated by her hand for him to take a seat. His eyes were everywhere, making a mental note. The lady sat at the table and began to quiz him about his work, adding for good measure that without the working classes the idle rich would be lost. Here was the first clue as to the reason for his ruse.

He thanked the lady and resumed sweeping the road. In a way he quite enjoyed the experience. A lot of people stopped and chatted.

When he returned to Wentworth, Deborah was as he had left her, nursing baby Andrew. After tea Freddie had a bath and tried to shave off his beard, but it was hopeless. Deb and Jane smiled, even Andrew started to cry when he got near to him. 'That was it,' he thought to himself, 'it's the barber in the morning.' He told Deb. what he was going to do.

"Thank goodness Freddie, I don't like you with a beard." The next morning it was the first thing he did and he found it an unusual experience. After it was done he felt his old self again. Even Deborah and Jane welcomed him as his old self. He had a kiss from both! Now he had to compose a preliminary report of how the ruse that was set up turned out. Was it a success or not? He was not allowed to post it but had to deliver it by hand to Richard, which to say the least was annoying.

The journey got off to a bad start. He missed his train, then two buses. This made up his mind to go to the garage where the Humber Snipe was having an overhaul. During the past weeks the car had slipped his mind. Freddie eventually arrived at the house somewhat flustered, met Richard who asked how things had gone. A nod was sufficient for an answer.

Before he left for Maidenhead about the car he went down to the canteen where he caused more commotion by not looking where he was going and bumping into a girl's tray, with her dinner finishing up on the floor. He apologised to the girl, turned around and left. His appetite had deserted him.

When he arrived at the garage he was greeted with the words "Hello guy, we've been trying to locate you. Your Humber has been ready for a couple of weeks now. We finally got the part we were searching for but she still won't start."

"How much do I owe you?"

"Seventeen quid, is that OK?"

"Yes, but just let me try and see if I can get her going." Well of course he did – it was the hidden switch. Freddie managed to scrape together the money and took a chance to get it to Wentworth unlicensed. His chances were good as by now ten days before Christmas it was dark by late afternoon. He took things easy and drove on to the house without incident. Tomorrow he would tax and insure and get new number plates. By noon the next day he was fully mobile. He had a car which to many working class men was only a distant dream and in the evening took Deborah out for a spin, stopping for a drink at a pub in Ascot. Deborah was in her mind taken back to India when Freddie was her driver and where unlike there she had to sit in the back, now she could sit close to him while he was driving.

After a few drinks she was back to her old vibrant self – happy, carefree and above all it seemed to him something had been released from her. What it was mattered not, he was just happy for her.

CHAPTER 41

Freddie was asked to attend a session of de-briefing at 10.30 the next day, to complement his report. He was ushered into a different room than on his previous visits.

Opening the proceedings one of the three men he had not seen before began, "Did you have any difficulty gaining entry to the house?"

"The lady was hesitant at first but said yes of course and gestured to the stairs – it is the first door on the left."

"What happened then?"

"I then pulled the chain and came downstairs. Every door on the landing was closed."

"As you came down, where was the woman?"

"She was waiting at the bottom in the hall. She then invited me into the kitchen for a cup of tea, which I accepted. After I had finished my drink I got up to leave. As I did so, she thrust these pamphlets, which I have here in my hand, and said, 'these might help you'." Freddie then gave them to one of the three men, adding that "On the way out the living room door was open and I noticed four or five large boxes. It looked to me, sir, that the boxes had only recently been delivered as they, as far as I could see, were put there in a hurry. I thanked the lady and resumed sweeping the road. About six houses down there was an alleyway which had some rubbish here and there so as nobody told me any details of what I had to do, I took it upon myself to clean it up. I think I got behind my time as this alleyway was long. It served some of the houses that had no side entrance. It also runs parallel to the road I was sweeping. When I got back to my truck an official was waiting. He was from the Highways Department and he asked me where I had been. He told me off saying all I had to sweep was the road and said, 'you're new here aren't you? I don't remember seeing you before'. And I told him the regular sweeper did not turn up for work. To me he was highly suspicious. It might be well, sir, if you had a word with him or about him!"

Quite out of the context about his report, the man in the centre said, "I think you have done very well young man and I think it is now time that we at least tell you who we are. I am Major General L. Elderfield." The next to be named was Inspector Marcham and the third was Lt Col. Wishton.

"Thank you Mr Radnor, you will be hearing from us. In the meantime we can act on your faultless report. We have much to go on. Carry on as usual, particularly at the technical college. That situation will cover you for any eventuality that may arise."

On leaving, Richard called him back and told him to wait. "Here, Fred just sign this. I'll fill it in," and then gave him an envelope. Freddie instinctively knew that it was money. There seemed more than usual. He boarded the first bus that came along. He had no idea where it would take him. He bought a ticket to the West End – all buses go there. He sat on the top deck and going through Bayswater looking out of the window he saw something he wished he hadn't. It was Deborah coming out of a pub with a man, or so he thought. He tried to convince himself he was mistaken and to make sure leapt off the bus at the traffic lights and went back to try and catch up with whoever it was he had seen. But there was no sign of them. He even went into the pub and made some enquiries but nothing came of it, even after trying all four bars. All he got was: "No I can't remember, we were quite busy."

Freddie said, "Well you're not busy now." Then a barmaid told him it was closing time but she did remember a very striking blonde with an RAF man.

"Thank you, miss." And at that point the landlord told him to leave.

CHAPTER 42

On the journey back to Wentworth he kept asking himself was it Deborah or was it a look-alike? What disturbed him most of all was the man in RAF uniform. It happened so quickly, the sighting, him scurrying back and going from bar to bar in the pub. Freddie decided to make for Wentworth. The train journey seemed to take a long time. He kept asking himself whether he should confront her or see how things panned out. But unknown to him and his concern there was no need as when he approached Wentworth there in the drive was an MG sports car and he knew it was not Devendra's car but her brother's by the colour.

When he entered as usual by the service door there were a lot of people waiting to greet him. Deb moved swiftly into his arms saying, "Darling, I don't know where to begin, I have lots of news to tell you."

"Well first introduce me to this RAF gentleman."

"You have met him before, it's Tommy Haldane who brought you the box of goodies I sent you from Germany."

"Oh of course, sir, I'm sorry, I must confess I am a bit confused today."

Then Deb said, "Tommy has brought us a Christmas hamper. Tommy and I casually met this morning and we went for a drink and a chat at a pub in Bayswater talking over old times." Freddie nearly keeled over. Deb said, "Have you been drinking?"

"No, no, it's personal." Changing the subject and as if it was not obvious he asked who the lady was.

Deb said, "This is Kathleen, the district nurse, who keeps an eye on Andrew and Jane. The final piece of news is that I have been offered a part in a Christmas pantomime starting on Boxing Day, so the company will be rehearsing every day." Breaking into all the talk, Nurse Kathleen said she must be on her way and said goodbye to everyone. She was only gone a few moments when she came back, saying she had a puncture on her bicycle. Freddie said he would see to it, but it was not a puncture but the valve was loose and it was soon ready to ride away.

Suddenly Deborah had changed and told Freddie to go to their flat and rest as he looked tired. He did not want telling twice. In the chair he fell asleep, waking only for Jane who had a cup of tea for him. Thanking her, Jane left. Freddie was called to come down as the evening meal was ready but he did not respond. Deb found him in bed and quickly 'phoned the nurse, asking her could she find a doctor as yet they had not registered with a GP. About ten minutes later the doctor arrived, accompanied by Nurse Kathleen and they found him only semi-conscious and after a routine examination decided to send for an ambulance.

In no time he was admitted to hospital, initially for overnight observation. Deborah was asked to leave after kissing Freddie on each cheek and was told to 'phone some time during mid-morning. She then realised that at that time she would be at rehearsals. When she got back to Wentworth Jane had been crying and this had an effect on Deb. They both slept uneasily and more than once one found the other downstairs drinking tea and smoking.

About 4am Deborah asked Jane if she thought Freddie had become ill over her and Tommy Haldane having a drink, but Jane dismissed that and said, "You did the right thing in telling your husband."

"No," said Jane. "It might be his work or something?" This hit Deborah as the only reason 'the beard', his first big mission! She convinced herself it could only be the reason. Jane nodded in agreement. That next morning Deborah left Wentworth to go to the theatre to begin rehearsals for the pantomime. In the mid-morning break she 'phoned the hospital as she was advised to do and was told there was no change in her husband's condition. She enquired if could she visit him that evening. The answer was no and she was told that she must adhere to the regulated visiting times, although she could 'phone morning and evening.

That evening Deborah's bed was a lonely place and she asked Jane would she sleep with her. Jane said, "Yes, but I must bring Andrew in as well in his cot." Both had a better night's sleep.

On arriving at the theatre the next day, the company was not happy with the production and they saw fit to bring in a bigger name. In turned out to be none other than the leader of the ENSA troupe from the time the troupe left England right through to India. He had the honourable rank of Captain. Coming face to face with him he called Deb all the nasty names he could think of, concluding with accusing her of being the equivalent of an army deserter. The company was rehearsing and everybody heard what he had to say as he shouted at her. Deborah did the only thing she could do and ran out of the building, grabbing her coat and handbag, crying for all she was worth. But where could she run and to whom? There was no Freddie Radnor now he was in hospital!

She found an ABC café and sat down in a corner out of the way having a cup of tea and a smoke, trying to decide what to do next. She decided to go to the Strand house in West London, if nothing else but to inform Richard what had happened and where Freddie was. She began to feel better because she had made a decision. Her luck had returned, Richard was there and she put him in the picture. He told her to leave things with him and if anyone was obstructive or awkward to let him know.

"We can always take care of any situation. We always put our personnel first," he told her. He even gave her his home 'phone number, as well as a kiss on her right cheek. He seemed to be enjoying the situation. He suggested to her that she go down to the canteen, have whatever she fancied then retire to the rest room until he came to tell her what his [Fred's] superiors would do, even if they did nothing. She took his advice and after an hour or some came to the rest room. Richard told her that arrangements were being made to have her husband transferred to a military hospital, as it was not uncommon in his condition. Also, she would be able to visit him at any time.

"You see Mrs Radnor we always take care of our people," and he suggested she go home and await any news. While escorting Deborah to the main doors, Richard remarked what a graceful, elegant walk she had. Her reply was that was a result of the training she had had for the ballet and she thanked him for the compliment. Then she was on her way.

Arriving back at Wentworth she found Jane putting up some Christmas decorations, as she did so nursing baby Andrew. She told Jane the latest news and told her she must write letters as well as cards to Freddie's parents and to her own. Christmas was not on her list of things to do. Nonetheless the holiday would do her good. It was then she realised how life would be more easy if she could drive and decided to make learning to do so her New Year's resolution. Her Freddie would teach her.

Deborah visited Freddie in the military hospital. He was placed in a room with just one bed so as to keep him from all the comings and goings in an open ward. She could not bear to see him lying there so did not stay long. On the way out the senior nurse asked her to come into her office. She asked Deborah if she knew of a girl or lady by the name of Denise, as her husband had called out her name on several occasions. Deb's reply was no but over the Christmas holiday she would try to remember. As she left the hospital grounds on a whim she decided to spend Christmas with her parents. When she did things like that it would more or less be the right decision. When she told Jane, Jane was very disappointed but understood. Deb also tried to contact Devendra but was told by her maid she and her brother with other friends were in Switzerland skiing. So that was that. Home to Mum and Dad. The quicker Christmas was over and a new year the better.

On Christmas Day she 'phoned the hospital. When she was put through to the ward the Sister said, "Prepare yourself for a pleasant shock, Mrs Radnor. This morning Fredddie was discovered sat up in bed wide-awake and asking for breakfast. Everyone including myself cannot understand it, but there it is."

"Did he ask after me?"

"No, he seems more concerned about his stomach than anything else. It's a pity it's Christmas Day, but unless you can get someone or a taxi to bring you here you will have to wait until tomorrow when the bus service starts."

Thanking the Sister, Deborah rang off and ran as fast as she could back home to her parents, who too were overjoyed. It was the best Christmas present she could have hoped for. Deborah could not sleep, the reason was she thought and worried. Why did Freddie not mention or ask after her?

When she arrived at the hospital, although it was Boxing Day, the senior nurse said, "Before you see your husband, Mrs Radnor, the ward doctor would like you to see him as he has something to tell you. Come with me, I will take you to his room." After the introductions and pleasantries, the doctor said that the Chief Medical Officer decided to call in a consultant who he knew personally three days ago, and after examining her husband came to the conclusion that Mr Radnor was the victim of a severe shock and had asked the doctor to ask you if you could suggest anything which might have contributed to his illness? Deborah said no, she had no idea. She did so but could not divulge his work to anyone, not even a doctor. She was at last taken to see her Freddie.

When she entered his room he was out of his bed, sat in an armchair in a service dressing gown. He stared at her at first then opened his arms and embraced her. After a few kisses Deborah looked around the room, spotted a chair and sat next to him, her left arm around his shoulder. She asked how he felt. "Oh, not too bad dear, I am being well looked after."

It was a typical hospital visit, neither could think of what to talk about. So Deb asked him, "What brought all this on?"

Freddie replied, "Do you really want to know?"

"Yes I do and so do the doctors."

"Well I will tell you. When I left the Strand the time was quarter to two. I got on the first bus that came along to get to central London. As the bus passed a pub in Bayswater I saw you and Tommy Haldane leaving the pub. I got out of my seat and jumped off to try and catch you but I saw you and Haldane drive off in his MG. Then I went into the pub and a barmaid confirmed you were both there for an hour or so. Then when I arrived back at Wentworth there was Haldane's MG, the same one and you know what happened when I arrived. Deborah, what is going on? It is the reason why I nearly fainted in Jane's kitchen. Are you having an affair with Haldane?"

On hearing this, her first reaction was calling out, "Oh my God, what can I say?" She screamed out and burst into tears, crying her heart out and becoming hysterical, saying, "No, no, no." Her head was bowed over her hands and she was muttering, "Oh what have I done? I am so sorry Freddie, my love." At this she fainted. At least she was in the right place to do so, a hospital.

A doctor and a nurse rushed into Freddie's room to help. Now it was her turn to go through what she had inflicted on her husband. Freddie left the room. As he did, the doctor who had been attending him took him to the day room and told him to stay there until things calmed down. He was in the room for about an hour when a nurse came in, accompanied by Deborah. She looked dreadful – the worst he had ever seen ever since he had met her. As by now the day room had other patients it was no place for a married couple to sort things out, so they were taken to another room, bare except for two hard chairs and a table.

So began the process to retrieve some sort of normality. Freddie spoke first, telling her how awful she looked, continuing by saying, "Deborah you are a very beautiful woman in fact too beautiful. I am a very lucky man to have you as my wife." They were the most wonderful words she had ever heard in her life. As one they both stood up and embraced and kissed as they had never done before, only interrupted by a knock on the door by the nurse carrying some refreshments and saying that Mr Radnor's doctor would be seeing him soon. Deborah's response to all of this was, "Please forgive me, please Freddie."

His reply was "Of course I do." He added, "When I get discharged we have to sort out our life and settle down as a normal man and wife, free from Devendra and others. We must get the cottage habitable as soon as we can." With that, Deb left but to where at that point in time she did not know on the bus heading toward London. Wentworth it had to be as all her belongings were there.

When she arrived Jane was overjoyed that Freddie was much better. Perhaps 1951, the new year, would herald a new start. While both were sat in the kitchen, Jane mentioned that Tommy Haldane had fixed a visit and before Deb could think of what to say, Jane said, "Tommy has asked me out to accompany him to a West End show and asked me to ask you would you mind sitting in to look after Andrew?"

At this Deborah said yes she would, but the very mention of his name made her angry and she told Jane that, "Tommy Haldane must not come into the house when I am here," as she never wanted to see or hear his name again.

"I will 'phone Freddie to tell him, Jane dear. It is best until Freddie is discharged. You must meet him away from Wentworth, not let him come and call for you in his car." Jane understood.

CHAPTER 43

Freddie was discharged from the hospital in the first week of the new year and was told to do nothing but relax and clear his mind of what had happened – to do some gardening or go for walks, get out into the fresh air. He took it upon himself to tidy up Wentworth's garden and grounds, getting the go-ahead from Devendra's agent with his blessing as it had got into a sorry state. One day as he was clearing a heap of last summer's fallen leaves he came across two unusual keys on a ring. Neither had been tarnished by the winter's elements so it was obvious the quality of the metal was exceptional.

Nobody in the household from Devendra down to Jane had said 'has anybody found a pair of keys?' or 'I have lost them'. His instinct told him they were special so he had put them in his pocket and told no-one. He asked Jane if she had the keys to the double garage doors as he could see through a window there was a large Atco lawnmower, which probably needed servicing for the coming summer. Jane said that the doors to the garage were sealed and were locked in the agent's office safe.

This gave Freddie a clue. He thought, in those double garages there was a secret of something and I bet these two keys are the clue. Nobody wanted it to be known that they were lost or missing, so he hid them and awaited developments. He mentioned the lawnmower to the agent who said he would be coming down to Wentworth anyway to inspect the property. "Also, I would like to meet you in person young man. Just a moment, I will look at my diary." The agent came back on the 'phone and said, "Will next Wednesday be all right?"

Freddie said, "Yes, sir, I will be here all day." Meanwhile, how was Deborah behaving? She was her normal self, always looking glamorous, self-confident and carefree. She herself had learned her lesson over the Tommy Haldane affair. It seemed to have brought her down to her responsibilities. Also Devendra was out of the way at least for the time being. What would make both their lives perfect, if there were such a thing, would be living in their own home, when Deb could put her talents in making it one and her falling for a child of her own. As for a home, the cottage she had bought him for his wedding present needed much work and money to be brought up to a standard which was acceptable for this point in time, halfway through the twentieth century. Freddie was having some difficulty with the council, owing to new building and planning laws introduced by the post-war government.

The agent arrived at Wentworth about mid-morning. Freddie made sure he was seen to be busy. The gentleman introduced himself as Mr Carter. They both walked round the grounds and Mr Carter was more than pleased with what Freddie had done and what he suggested to Mr Carter that needed to be repaired. Among his suggestions for repair was the rotting window casement at the side of the garage. At this point Deb came out and asked them both in for coffee. Mr Carter could also look inside, all of which made a good impression on Mr Carter. Eventually Mr Carter got around to unsealing the interim door that led from the hall into the garage. There were no cars inside and Freddie went straight to the Atco lawnmower. He removed the cover and in doing so uncovered a wooden strong box next to it. He recognised its origin – it was made in India, and well made at that – with two wide metal brackets on each corner and an interior lock. While Mr Carter was doing other things, Freddie tried one of the two keys he had found and lo and behold it fitted. He could do no more as Mr Carter said, "I will open the main doors so you can get the mower outside," and that was all he could do. The garage was locked and sealed again.

Deborah invited Mr Carter into the room next to the kitchen for coffee. He accepted the offer with pleasure. While taking coffee, Mr Carter noticed Deborah drinking a glass of whisky but said nothing, but thought all the more. Completing his work, Deborah again invited Mr Carter and Freddie for a drink before he left. Deborah told him that an RAF friend brought it back from West Germany. Freddie meanwhile put away the mower. When he returned poor Mr Carter was highly flushed and confessed to Freddie he had taken advantage of his wife's hospitality. Whether Deb had noticed or not was uncertain. Freddie told the agent that he should not drive in his condition. Mr Carter agreed as he had to keep out of trouble or his business would suffer. Freddie suggested that he would drive him home or wherever he was going. Mr Carter thought for a moment and agreed to Freddie's advice, adding, "You'd best drive me home and explain to my wife what happened." Deborah never said a word.

Mr Carter lived in North London and at a point about half way Mr Carter asked Freddie to stop as he wished to have a word with him. He began by saying, "I'm very impressed by you, Mr Radnor, you seem a very genuine man." And in the next sentence he told Freddie that he was a trained and a qualified medical doctor but had decided to give up the medical profession to pursue another career which appealed to him, which is why he had set up his agency. He had seen enough blood while serving in the Army Medical Corps during the war and he said, "Try and get your wife off drinking or at least cut it down, otherwise she will die young." Freddie did not want telling as he had already come to the same conclusion. Mr Carter said, "Is there anything bothering your wife?"

"Yes there is, she desperately wants a child of her own but so far she has not, or should I say we have not been successful."

"Well young man, perhaps I might make a few suggestions, being an ex-doctor. First feed yourself up with as much protein as you can, i.e. eggs, meat, particularly steak. Secondly, try to get your wife to relax. She may be falling into the trap of trying too hard. Catch her on the hop. Don't wait for bedtime. Don't give her time to think about it. Anyway, it's worth a try. But I will leave it up to you. So let's get home and face my problem – my wife."

Freddie drove into Mr Carter's driveway. Leaving him in the car, he rang the doorbell. His wife opened it and she panicked but Freddie immediately reassured her it was nothing to worry about and in a few words told Mrs Carter what had happened. Her response was one of relief and all was forgiven. He spent about an hour there before leaving for home. Mr Carter's words to him as he left were, "Thank you. I won't forget you," and he gave him a fiver and his business card.

CHAPTER 44

Freddie made his way back to Central London before catching a train home. After treating himself to something nice in Fortnum & Masons, he had just passed the new French Tourist Office when he heard someone running in high-heeled shoes calling, "Freddie, Freddie, it's me, it's me, Denise." He turned around and it was none other than Denise, the French girl who was the one who initiated or seduced him to the pleasures of sex for the first time in his life. They embraced and kissed in the view of everyone in Piccadilly. Arm in arm they walked back to the tourist and travel centre where she was employed. Denise sat Freddie down and said, "Please wait a moment, mon amour, I will be back soon."

Freddie was overcome at seeing her again and he smiled to himself thinking 'let's hope Deborah was not on that bus as I was on that terrible day in Bayswater'. Denise came back and told him her supervisor had granted her the rest of the day off in view of what had happened. They left and she guided him to a small restaurant where they could talk. While in the restaurant they brought up the subject of how their respective lives had panned out. Denise said the second time she saw him at the airfield – when all she could do was wave to him – she had something to tell him, but could not leave the plane as she had to close the aircraft's door. Did he remember?

"Yes I remember only too well. What was it?"

"I will tell you later when you are with your wife." When Freddie got back to Wentworth he wanted to tell Deborah his news but before he could she said to him that Tommy Haldane and Jane had become engaged and they were both very happy. "Isn't that great, dear?" Freddie could do no more but agree and embraced and kissed her. He then told Deb what had happened on his way along Piccadilly. For a moment Deb dropped her excitement but when he said, "Denise would like both of us to come up to town for dinner," her mood changed to what it had been a moment before.

"That would be nice and it would make a pleasant evening out," Deb answered. The venue was arranged by Denise. It was dinner at a newly-opened French restaurant and a table was booked for 7.30. Denise was already seated at the table alone. This immediately put Deborah in a state of unease, seeing her as a threat, asking herself what was this intruder up to? Denise planted a kiss on both cheeks for Freddie, but this gesture was tactically resisted by Deborah offering her hand instead. It did not go unnoticed.

All of a sudden a tall man appeared. Denise introduced him as Roland Demonde, her friend. Deborah soon lost this feeling of insecurity, as if within her she had switched off like a light bulb and the atmosphere changed. After one of the most notable dinners Freddie had experienced, Roland asked to be excused. Freddie went to leave his chair to do the same, but was persuaded by Denise to wait as she had something to tell him, and most important of all in the presence of his wife. Then Denise started to cry. After a few seconds she said:

"Freddie, my amour, I have to tell you that because of the liaison in your room – a night I will never forget –

I became ..." sobbing again ... " I gave birth to a baby boy nine months later. What I am saying is that, unknown to you up until now, you are the father of a beautiful boy."

At this Denise broke down. Deborah got out of her chair and disappeared to the ladies' room, saying nothing. Freddie's eyes welled up and at the same time he was consoled by Denise.

"Please don't cry. You have told me the best and most wonderful thing I have heard," Freddie told her and enquired, "Where is the child?" Denise quickly assured him he was in good hands. He was being brought up by her Mamma and Papa on their farm in central France. When Deborah returned to her seat, all she said was, "I suppose you want some maintenance money from my husband? Is that it?"

With that last remark Freddie had had enough of Deborah's attitude and told her to say nothing more. Deborah saw it as a rebuke and in a public place at that. This time leaving her seat, she left the restaurant. Roland was returning and could see for himself what the situation was. He did not take his seat but aimed for the entrance in the wake of Deborah and within a few moments brought her back, clutching her upper left arm.

"Here Monsieur Radnor is your wife. She is now in your hands. Please take her back outside, everybody is looking. I will settle the bill and then console Denise," who was, by now, herself in tears. On the journey back to Wentworth neither said a word or even looked at each other. Both stared out of the bus and train windows, taking advice from that old but true saying, 'least said soonest mended'. Not a word was said even when walking from the station.

On arriving home Deborah reached for the whisky bottle and cigarettes. Freddie went upstairs and sat in the room where they had spent their first night as man and wife. Now what to do? Wentworth was the only place he himself, Deborah and Jane had to live. All three were trapped. Freddie wanted to go home to his mother but it was impossible as he was employed by Devendra's agent, Mr Carter, albeit part-time. For the moment he slept on the situation. In fact he slept in Devendra's bed. Surprisingly he had a good night. He was woken by Jane with a cup of tea. All she said was "Good morning." She too must have realised something had happened. And where Deborah was and what she was doing he did not care.

Freddie decided to get in the Humber and in turn to report to the Strand, the technical college and finally Mr Carter, telling the latter what had happened the previous evening and that he would like to leave Wentworth as soon as possible. Mr Carter's reply was, "It is not your fault, Fred. You have proved you are capable. It is your wife who cannot conceive and that is the cause of her actions. It is ruining her life. Unless it happens she must accept the fact she cannot have children. Now I must ask or even beg you to return to Wentworth, if only for you to be there. I did not like the idea of one woman being alone there, let alone two. I can authorise you to have complete freedom of the place. Treat it as though it was your own. I feel I can trust you."

At this last remark, it convinced Freddie to do what Mr Carter had requested, until he was informed to the contrary. Driving along the A30 towards Wentworth he wondered what the atmosphere would be, or even was Deborah still there? He soon found out. She had hit the bottle and was drunk and helpless. Jane even had taken the decision to call her own doctor as she herself was frantic and asked Freddie did he mind.

"No, Jane, you have done me a favour." The doctor rang the bell and was taken by Freddie to where Deborah was out for the count. She looked terrible. The doctor could not only smell her breath but noticed the bottle of whisky by her side. It was just over half empty. He needed to do no more examining of her, she was just drunk and he told Freddie he was with his permission to send for an ambulance to take her to hospital, adding, "It will give me some time to consult a fellow doctor as to what to do." Within half an hour she was gone and both Jane and himself embraced, crying. Even baby Andrew began to cry as if the little fellow knew something was wrong.

Although it was not visiting hours, Freddie went to the hospital to enquire how Deborah was but was brushed aside by a formidable matron, whose tart reply was, "She is in an induced sleep and when she wakes up will have a deserved hangover." At this last remark, Freddie blew his top, throwing a bunch of keys, just missing the matron and shouting at her and at the same time suggesting for her own sake to call a senior doctor. What in fact Freddie was doing was pulling rank. He already had his pass in the palm of his hand. Within a few seconds a doctor in his white coat intervened and overruled the matron and took him to see his wife, who was in a small side ward, lying so still on her back she could be already dead, but somehow as always she kept her attractive looks. He put his head down to her, kissed and stroked her cheek and whispered, "I love you, please get better for me, please."

Then Freddie withdrew and left. If this was not enough, Devendra had been to Wentworth and upset Jane while he was at the hospital. That was the last thing he wanted but he could do nothing about her. Like a spider on a good day, she had everyone in her power and this made Freddie determined to break free from her. The cottage was now his number one priority. Jane told Freddie that Devendra had been very cold and informal towards her and went straight to the garage, breaking the seal to the door, with what she couldn't say, and was in there for about ten minutes alone. He went straight to see for himself, but could not see anything had changed, but he thought she would not have gone in there for nothing. He turned round and left, deciding to 'phone Mr Carter, who said, "Just leave it locked."

CHAPTER 45

Meanwhile, Deborah was on the way to recovery and on his latest visit to her he was informed that she would be discharged. But before he left the hospital he was literally waylaid by a female doctor who was a psychiatrist from a mental hospital and ushered Freddie into a small room. She introduced herself and told him that someone had anonymously suggested that his wife needed some help, if only to get her off her addiction to alcohol. Also, she said that she had spoken to her twice and had come to the conclusion there was something deep down which was triggering the drinking habit and, with his permission she should be admitted to the hospital where she was practising. Without any hesitation Freddie said, "No, no," but asked that if his wife needed this treatment could she have it at home?

"That is not allowed Mr Radnor, but if you can bring her to my consulting room once a week I can list her as an out-patient. How does that sound?"

"Well I must talk it over with Deborah and if she agrees, so will I."

As he sat in the Humber, going through his mind was who was the anonymous person? When he returned to Wentworth, Jane said she was going out shopping and would be gone for about an hour. This he saw as an opportunity now that Devendra had herself broken the seals of the internal door into the garage. He checked all external doors to the house to make sure he would not be disturbed. Once inside the garage he made straight for the box that he had discovered when previously he removed the cover near the lawnmower. He opened it and found another smaller one inside, identical in every way and tried to open it with the second key. He found it fitted, turned it and inside was a virtual treasure chest containing one- and five-pound notes, jewellery, rings, gems, and necklaces. Some were very similar to the one he had found in Deborah's handbag on that fateful day in India where Deborah and himself had realised he was in love with her. Life since that day had changed the way he looked at the world. Now he had no scruples about anything, so he helped himself to a few pound and also five-pound notes, not bothering to count them, then also to a handful of jewellery. He closed the two boxes, locked them and half covered them as he had previously found them, disturbing nothing. He locked the connecting door and gave the keys to Jane when she returned. As for the two box keys, he would throw them into a river. In the meantime. Freddie went back to the college and resumed his duties now on a daily basis, sometimes going undercover and tailing someone who was under suspicion.

CHAPTER 46

It was now spring of 1951, a year of great activity everywhere you looked. There was another war, this time in Korea, and to top everything two members of the Foreign Office, Burgess and Maclean, had gone missing. MI5 and the papers were speculating they had defected to Russia but were yet not sure! It was a busy time. The psychiatrist had transformed Deborah back to normality and by now she again shared the marital bed. But one night around 3am Deborah woke him up, not intentionally, but by making a noise in the bathroom and her bedside lamp was switched on. As she emerged in the half light he could see her figure through her nightdress. This aroused him and as she went to get into bed he grabbed her and lifting her nightdress up to her neck he gently entered her. In a matter of seconds, it was all over. It was what both needed. They were both still in love, even if there was doubt that it had in fact ever left them. Freddie was awakened the next morning by Deborah standing beside the bed with a cup of tea, fully dressed and looking radiant.

The four sessions Deborah had with Dr Williams brought her back from the brink, but who was the person who was responsible? Someone who knew the situation Deborah was in. Dr Williams wrote to Freddie asking could they meet alone, emphasising that it was in a professional capacity and concerning his wife.

This was accepted by him. They met in a small room at the hospital and the doctor began by saying that it would be unprofessional to disclose what his wife had told her during the past four weeks, but she was prepared to reveal to him that his wife was insecure in herself and was obsessed that one day he would find another person to love. Also, she was concerned about his work and that something would happen to him.

"You're in an awkward position, aren't you, Mr Radnor?" Freddie had to agree. At this point their meeting ended and, on shaking hands, Dr Williams said, "How are your Indian lilies?" slightly breaking her lips into a wry smile and then said:

"Goodbye, I'm sure we shall meet again." After that it was obvious to Freddie that Dr Patricia Williams was a member of the Secret Service and she alone in the capacity of her profession would be very useful to the Service, i.e. the Strand would be able to know what was going on in a suspect's mind. The Service had a specialist for use on any assignment.

Having Deborah back on an even keel, Freddie had decided his life had to change. He had, as it were, come to a fork in the road but there were no signposts to show him the way. At times Deborah would notice him completely day-dreaming, learning day-by-day how to approach him without upsetting the applecart. Both were, or had been, skating on thin ice.

A few days later Freddie was given an assignment in a Berkshire village and told not to travel in his own car but to use the bus. On the journey the bus passed through Maidenhead, the town where he and Deborah had said so many hellos and goodbyes, particularly the last one. As he gazed out of the bus window it stopped for one reason or another and on the opposite side of the road was the Bear Hotel, where he had waited for Deborah and then he suddenly remembered the gentleman who then invited Freddie to join him for a drink and during their conversation had advised Freddie that if he wanted to make a decent living to get into buying and selling.

'That's it, that's it, that's the answer. How strange,' he thought to himself. It was as if fate had guided him there. Freddie, without a moment's hesitation, decided to find a suitable place and set himself up in business. His assignment completed, he returned to Wentworth in a more buoyant mood. He told Deborah what he had decided to do and she, in turn, was thrilled and in full agreement. She also suggested to him, "Why don't you ask Mr Carter to help you find a shop or yard to start you up?" At this last remark, she corrected herself and bettered 'you' for 'us'. "Just the two of us and nobody else."

After breakfast the next morning he did just that. Mr Carter said he would get back to him in a few days, as, at the moment, he was very busy because of the change of government. That same day the postman put through the letterbox some mail for the threesome living at Wentworth. Among some for Deborah was one in particular. It was ribboned red, white and blue and with French postage stamps and the words 'Par Avion'. It was addressed to Mrs D. Radnor. She showed it unopened to Freddie who said, "Well go on, open it!"

On doing so Jane and Freddie looked uninterested but they were even though they were opening their own mail. Deborah interrupted by saying it was from Denise. Also a recent photograph of her baby boy, now aged four years, and written on the back was his name 'Frederique'. She gave the photograph to Freddie saying nothing other than:

"I am going to our room to read the letter," which was enclosed for her.

One of the letters was addressed to both of them. It was an invitation from Mr & Mrs Carter to come to their home for lunch on Easter Sunday. When Deborah came down from their room, her face spoke volumes and she gave him Denise's letter to read but he said, "No," as the letter was hers and hers alone. But what he did see was that the letter was typed. She asked him again to read it but the answer was the same. Deborah did no more but light a cigarette and with the same match set the letter alight into a large ashtray saying as the flames consumed it, "I do not want to hear any more about that woman or her child, whether it is yours or not."

Jane, who witnessed all of this, interjected with, "If this is a sample of married life you can keep it! I am myself having second thoughts about getting married. There is something about Tommy [Haldane] I'm not sure about." Now it was Jane's turn to be rebuked, reminding her about not mentioning his name again. This was too much for Freddie to handle and he went out into the garden. Deborah came out to join him and there and then he told her he was leaving Wentworth.

"Where are you going Freddie? Are you taking me with you?"

"Yes, if you want to come with me. If not, I am going home to Mother."

"Well if that is the case I will go home to my parents, if only to get some peace. There are too many people in our lives. Come back inside and let's have a drink and see what we can come up with."

"OK, dear, that's the best idea I've heard for a long time."

CHAPTER 47

Deborah apologised to Jane, who dismissed the apology saying she understood. Then Freddie and Deborah went up to their rooms, poured themselves a drink, lit up and began to pack all of their belongings into anything they could find. When Deb said, "Dearest, we are leaving here but where are we going? Have you thought where we are actually going to?"

"Yes, we're going to our cottage, your wedding present to me, but I regard it as ours. It is not any worse than that hovel you lived in over the café in France. We will have some jolly good times, me doing all the woodwork and you putting your touch into the furnishings. As far as tonight, we'll find a hotel to sleep in."

Her face lit up with joy and she kissed him and embraced him, putting her hand into the top of his trousers and downward. Without hardly opening their eyes, they began undressing each other, while walking backwards towards the bed, which had not yet been made. Both entered it, with Freddie naked and Deborah clad only in a white singlet vest which he rolled up over those two sumptuous breasts, all the time caressing her. Afterwards both were completely exhausted and never moved for some half an hour. Deborah heard a knock on their door and called out, "Who is it?"

"It's me, Jane, are you all right?"

"Yes, I'll be down in a moment. I have something to tell you." So Jane left. If she knew or guessed what they had been up to, this did not trouble them.

Deb gave Freddie a nudge to wake him up, imploring him to get dressed before everything they had decided to do had lost its momentum. He told her to go down and tell Jane what was happening.

While Freddie was dressing, she sneaked a whisky to give her Dutch courage. It was an errand she did not want to do, but, after downing the drink and following it with a cigarette, she went downstairs and with no hesitation told Jane what she and Freddie had decided to do.

Jane's response surprised Deborah when she said, "I think I would do the same if I were in your position. That is why I am engaged to you know who. I made up my mind some time ago to grab the first man who came along. Well good luck to you both, but keep in touch. You might get an invitation to our wedding, whenever that is. But don't go for a while, I can give you a bundle of household items; they'll give you a start wherever you go."

The Humber was full to the brim and Deborah even had some items on her lap. They said their goodbyes and off they went to begin a new phase in their lives, determined to be just the two of them. All they wanted was each other. On the journey neither could stop talking about all of the incidents from India and their subsequent meetings in Maidenhead. Deborah remarked that, looking back, it had been the happiest of times for her, even mentioning the day when she waited for him to arrive at the station when she nearly stopped him boarding his train. She told him she wished she had done so and both could have run away and disappeared to anywhere where life or fate would have taken them. Freddie said he had wished she had come running down the platform steps calling out, "Freddie darling, don't leave me, don't leave me," but of course she had not.

The journey to their cottage seemed to go so quickly they were soon outside it. It looked so sad and forlorn as if to say, "Please come in and make me your home."
After unloading the Humber, they sat on whatever they could find and composed a list of what they had to do and buy, keeping it simple. Freddie first was to contact Mr Carter to tell him the situation. When he did so, by 'phone, he was very put out but said always put your personal life above everything else. Deborah did the writing of the necessary letters. They went to Mr Brown's yard to see what he could do for them in the way of furniture. He didn't have much to offer but came up with a brilliant idea but, for some reason, he didn't tell them what it was. He said, "Drive me to your cottage and let me have a look."
On the journey both wondered why, but when they arrived Mr Brown said, "Good, you have room at the side, so you can get one in there and have space to spare."
"Well what is it then?" they asked.
Mr Brown said, "A caravan." Deborah embraced Mr Brown and Freddie, in between jumping up and down like an excited child. Mr Brown took them to the showground which was only ten minutes' drive away. Why had it never occurred to them, it was the perfect solution? A new beginning in their lives had been born. There were only three models to choose from and Deb. would have liked the largest of the trio, but Mr Brown said it would not fit into the space at the side of their cottage, so the deal went through.

While all of this was taking place, Freddie thought in vain of everything regarding the money and jewellery stashed away. With Deb's 'nod' he opted for just the deposit and the rest on hire purchase over two years. Deb caught on what he was doing and his motive – 'always plead at first that you have not much money and people will then help you for the right reasons'. Within a week the caravan was delivered, jacked up and ready to live in. During that week Mr Carter requested they give him time to sort out a replacement for Freddie so they commuted between Maidenhead and Wentworth, just to sleep, then drove back to Maidenhead. Everything was falling into place.

One morning in that week Deborah said to Freddie, "Darling, don't get too excited but I am ten days over my time, let us hope it is not a false alarm." He was surprised and pleased, if only for her as it might help her to mature, keep her off the drink and be content with life. It seemed to him their life had come full circle after all they had been through. Getting close to Maidenhead, hearing all of this, Freddie lost his concentration and nearly ran into the back of another car, stopping just inches away. The incident brought him back to reality.

While in a quiet moment to himself, his eyes focused on a wooden box containing items of no importance, but it reminded him of the two boxes in Devendra's garage which he had half plundered and realised for the first time in his life he had been a thief. He regretted what he had done but it was done and he could now only do one of two things to put that right – throw it into the river or use it. He could tell no-one, not even his wife. He decided on the latter course. The only worrying thing was the five-pound notes. A working man earning less than five pounds a week seldom saw, let alone possessed one. Using them on a daily basis would arouse suspicion. He sought something or someone to blame for his uncharacteristic lapse in just putting his hand in the strong box at Wentworth and grabbing as much as his right hand could hold.

In the end he blamed his recruitment and training on the Strand. Doing this blaming game somehow relieved him from any more guilt. As for the jewellery, for the time being he would have to hide it somewhere safe. It could not be in the cottage as when it was being renovated much would be disturbed. He could not find a solution. He just had to be careful. As for the five-pound notes, he unpicked a part of a jacket and spread them evenly in the lining. Now what he had to do was every so often and in a different bank in a different place ask one of the counter staff if they could split this five-pound note into an assortment of change, telling them he had done some work for a gentleman and this was how he had been paid. Making small talk while the man was carrying out his request, it worked every time. He then hid most of the ten shilling and pound notes on the underside of an old table that was left behind in the cottage, sandwiched between a sheet of plywood – an old trick he had learned during the war when black market food was hidden.

It worked well for Freddie until all of it was converted. He put some in the Post Office savings bank each week, giving the appearance that Freddie Radnor was a thrifty working man.

CHAPTER 48

Easter was only two weeks away and, by the time it came, their home at the caravan was ready. Everyone who knew them, from the Strand to both their parents in turn, were inquisitive as to how a caravan looked inside. When they did visit, all remarked how well Deborah looked. She was absolutely blooming. Everyone put it down to the fact she was more settled and as for Freddie, he looked a little under the weather. When some enquired as to his well-being, be brushed them off with, "It's this cottage, there is so much to be done." But he himself knew the reason – he had become a common thief and a cheat. Also as a result all of this sudden wealth of which he had dreamt he would never have, he realised he would never be short of means and money. He had to be wary of getting caught and ending up in prison, like Ginger!

Mr and Mrs Carter invited them to Easter lunch. They arrived at noon and Deborah got to know Phyl Carter, even helping set the table, while Freddie was shown around Harry's collection of orchids. The occasion turned out to be a wonderful day, finishing with a game of solo whist. A friendship was born. On leaving, Harry's last words to Freddie were:
"I will do my best to find you a suitable shop or other premises so you can start up in your business. Leave Wentworth to me."

A few weeks later Deborah had some wonderful news. She told Freddie that the Doctor had confirmed she had successfully conceived and if all went well she could expect the birth in the autumn. Their eventful life which had begun with him offering her his hand when he drove her to the NAAFI store in India, was now blossoming. They decided in the meantime to make the most of what time was left before their child was born.

Things and events in that year 1951 meant much was going on. The Festival of Britain for one. As regards life in general, Deborah and Freddie had settled into some sort of routine. That was until one day in June. Freddie came home from work to find Deb had been smoking heavily – the evidence was in two ashtrays. Before he could ask if there something the matter, she said Mr Carter and an Indian gentleman had called. Mr Carter introduced him as the solicitor of Devendra and her brother, who looked after their affairs in England. He spoke perfect English and asked her whether she had had any correspondence in any form, be it letters, postcards, or anything? Had she met her say for lunch? Deborah said no, nothing, but she was a person who just on a whim would do something, go somewhere, then turn up out of the blue as if nothing had happened.

Mr Carter said he was asking because it was two months since anyone had seen or heard from either of them and, he was concerned, as he wanted her to sign some papers. Also her bank account was in overdraft and he needed more authority to pay her bills and settle her accounts, including Mr Carter's fee. Deborah said no, quite convincingly, without hesitation and the two visitors left saying, "Goodbye, but if you do hear from them please let either of us know." She said she would.

Freddie was a bystander in all this and was glad he was only that, just saying to her not to worry.

"In your condition, sweetheart, it isn't wise." She agreed.

All through their lives it seemed the two would never be without conflict or interruption. They knew too many and found themselves entwined in other people's lives. This situation came to a head when one evening the two men called again. Their mission was to ask would they both consider moving back to Wentworth. The answer was still no. Freddie said sorry to Harry Carter as he was a friend. Harry nodded back.

The solicitor, whom Freddie took an instant dislike to, then asked could he recommend someone to live at Wentworth in the meantime. Freddie said, "Yes, an ex-RAF officer, Tommy Haldane, as he is engaged to Jane."

Then he said to the Indian gentleman, "Would you please leave us alone now unless it is very important. You can contact Haldane through his fiancée."

Freddie shook Harry's hand but did not offer to do so to the solicitor, nor he in return. Then off they drove in a Rolls Royce Phantom, driven by the solicitor. He was obviously doing very well for himself. When he returned inside, Deborah embraced him saying how pleased she was that he had not been tempted by the offer and adding, "How could Tommy Haldane take on Wentworth while he's still in the RAF?" Freddie said that he knew he could as he got into some trouble and was asked to resign his commission, which he had done. "When did you hear all about this Freddie?"

"Last week, Richard told me. Let's just leave it at that."

For the next few weeks all they did, who they met and where they went suited both of them. At last they had what was their aim. At weekends Freddie got two of his students to get the cottage up-to-date, using new materials that were coming on to the market. Deborah answered an advert for a part-time assistant in a dress shop.

Life was great. It could not last of course. In June Harry Carter visited them one evening alone, saying he had some terrible news, particularly for Deborah. He told her to sit down and with a cigarette, and if there was a glass of brandy or whisky. She knew instinctively it was about Devendra and she was right. Harry told them that two bodies had been found by a hunter at the bottom of a ravine in the Alps, together with a sports car. It had for the past months been camouflaged by snow which had now melted. The bodies were of Devendra and her brother. It was certain who they were because the English number plate was registered in the Prince's name. For the moment that was all he could tell them.

Deborah, surprisingly at first, took the news very calmly. As for Freddie, he showed nothing, just saying, "How sad, let's hope they died quickly."

Harry said, "The post-mortem should throw light on that." Deborah's reaction to this news surprised both Harry and Freddie. It was a combination of relief and indifference. Bidding his farewell, Harry said, "Keep a close eye on her, she might do something when she has had time to take it all in. She might go off, take to the bottle or whatever. Do not let her dwell on it. Above all try and please her." Freddie took this advice to heart because if anyone knew Deborah it was he. He need not have worried about complying with Harry's advice. If anything she was carefree, as if a burden had been lifted from her shoulders. For the next two weeks he made sure she would be in somebody's company, even the Strand kept an eye on her while he was at the college. One evening Freddie could not restrain his silence over Devendra's death and he came out with it, whether it was the right time or not.

Deborah said, "No, not now dear, perhaps one day I will. Just let's get on with our lives and look forward to our coming child." He was pleasantly surprised at her attitude and wise reply, so he left well alone. If it had not been for Harry Carter, they would not have heard any more about Devendra and her brother's accident or their funeral. Both bodies were flown back to India, after which all of their affairs, their wills, Wentworth, and the property in London were sorted out. There was no need for Deborah or Freddie to become involved.

In the meantime Jane and Tommy Haldane were left to live and maintain Wentworth.

CHAPTER 49

Nineteen fifty-one was a glorious summer. They both made the most of it, sometimes going twice a day to the park.

At the beginning of December Deborah was due to give birth to their child. She was very large, so big that sometimes she would not venture out in daylight, only in the evenings.

The hospital and the health authorities decided that on the 14th of that month Deborah had to go into the maternity ward to stay as their caravan was not suitable if the child suddenly decided to be born. In the end it made sense and the next day Freddie drove her there, saw her in and told her all the loving things he could think of and left. When he arrived home a feeling came over him, one of which he had not experienced before.

He realised Deborah was not there to greet him and his eyes welled up. Lighting a cigarette, the depth of his love for her came to the fore. Now it was his turn to cry out as Deborah had done in the DC3 when she left India, seeing him wave to her standing by the Humber on that day when she and her husband left India.

So in the evening he went out and sought company in the saloon bar of the Bear Hotel. As he stood at the bar, a woman who was well dressed and good looking approached him.

"Hello, stranger, all alone are you?"

"Yes I am at the moment. I'm just going to have another drink. Can I buy you one?"

"Yes, thanks. I would like a gin and tonic, ice and lemon, please." When the drinks came they sat down and talked about things in general. Then the landlord called, "Last orders, please." Freddie ordered another round then it was time to leave – it was closing time. Out on the street, which was the A4, heavy lorries were proceeding to the London markets. They walked towards a colonnade of shops where they stopped. They exchanged names. Hers was Phyllis. Then she said, "I live over one of these, would you care to come up for a nightcap?"

Freddie replied, "Thank you but no. I must make a 'phone call to the hospital. My wife is expecting our baby."

Phyllis said, "Oh, you don't want anything else then?"

He said, "No, Phyllis, but thank you for your company," and gave her two pound notes.

She said, "That's not necessary," but he insisted. More pleasantries were exchanged and they bid each other goodnight.

As Freddie approached the caravan in the darkness he could see a tall figure coming towards him. It turned out to be a policeman who said, "Good evening sir, I don't suppose you're a Mr F. Radnor are you?"

"Yes I am. What is it you want?"

"Well I have been instructed to tell you to go to the maternity hospital as soon as you can as your wife is in some difficulty and is calling out for you. Those who are attending her think it's wise for you to do so."

Freddie did no more but get in the Humber and raced through the streets of Maidenhead to the hospital. When he arrived he never even bothered to switch the engine off but ran inside. Remembering where the ward was he ran straight to it. He could hear babies crying but was stopped in his tracks by Matron who told him he was the father of twins, a boy and a girl. But his wife was not well. "She has had a difficult time and make sure you see her first, before you see the babies. It is the custom. Please follow me and I'll take you to her."

At first glance he could hardly recognise her. It was obvious she had had a tough time. For a moment all he could do was stand at the foot of her bed. He was at a loss as to what to say or do, but suddenly Deborah, probably sensing his presence, opened her eyes and gave him the most wonderful of smiles. He rushed forward, kissed and embraced her saying, "Darling, what have I done to you?"

She replied, "Freddie Radnor, you have fulfilled my dream. It is what you have always done for me, ever since you put out your hand when we first met." That was all she could manage, falling out of his arms and dropping fast asleep.

Freddie enquired at a desk what he had to do, apart from informing her parents and his own. He was told he had to register their births with the Registry Office, but first he had to choose names. But there was no need to rush, the hospital had their own records. Both families were overjoyed, but when he returned to their home pinned on the door of the caravan was a note which read: 'Will Mr F.W. Radnor go to the maternity hospital as soon as you can.' He got straight back in the Humber and pushed the engine as far as he dared. When he arrived, frantically running down to where Deborah was, in the corridor confronting him were the Matron, the Doctor and another man.

"What is wrong? What has happened?" He was informed that his baby boy had died, in spite of all their efforts to save him. "We are so sorry. We have told your wife and she has taken it badly. She's under sedation and we suggest you stay here to be with her when she comes out of her enforced sleep." Freddie could do no more but do as they said.

He was sitting in the chair which was provided for him. To say it was uncomfortable was an understatement. He kept moving about in it, getting up and down, then walking about saying to himself, "Come on Deborah, please wake up." Another hour had passed when at last she started to move. It took another hour, or so it seemed, for her to be fully conscious. When she was, she just looked at him, her eyes and mouth told him everything. Both did not say a word and after waiting all that time he turned around, picked up his hat and coat and walked away, being chased by a nurse who was on duty pleading for him to return. But he said, "No, just leave me alone." He got into the Humber – the model which was responsible for all his torments but also a few pleasures since that fateful day at Maggadore when he was called into the Section Office – and drove off into the darkness.

CHAPTER 50

Driving towards Maidenhead, Skindles Hotel was not far away so he drove in, parking next to a Bentley. Going inside he just had time to order a double whisky before it was closing time. Turning around to find a seat, who should be in front of him but Phyllis from the Bear.

"Hello," she said, "you look terrible."

She already had a drink in her hand, so they sat down on a long couch which was more comfortable than the one in the hospital. She enquired how things were but she knew something was terribly wrong. Freddie was about to tell her when the hotel manager told them they must leave and, making a snide remark, he said, "You've found one then!"

At this Phyllis threw the rest of the drink into his face and, for good measure, so did Freddie, and both left. He offered her a lift to her flat which she accepted. When they arrived, she invited Freddie to come up for some supper. He readily agreed as he had not eaten all day. What she made him was most welcome. Afterwards they both sat and talked, which was dominated by Deborah's last two days and particularly about the loss of his son. She plied him with drink and his tongue was loose. Too loose, as he told her he was employed by the Security Service which he should not have done. But to his amazement, Phyllis came out with, "How are your Indian lilies?" This revelation relaxed him and made him feel better.

He was coming out of his depressive mood. He then stood up and inviting her to do the same, he embraced and kissed her and in return she asked him to stay the night. He did not want asking twice and she showed him into a small bedroom. Phyllis told him this was her private room. The large one was for her clients. She closed the door and said, "We will sleep here tonight and I will take most of your troubles away, at least for tonight!"

As she undressed, fully aroused, she washed herself, indicating she was clean. Out went the lights except for a sultry blue one, and she showed him some tricks of her trade.

"This one is on the house," she said. Eventually, they broke off and Freddie fell into a deep, deep sleep. But, before Phyllis did the same she lay on her back looking into the void of the room, saying to herself how wonderful it was that, not for the first time by any means, she had relieved a man of all his wearisome troubles and for this one beside her tomorrow was far away. She turned over towards his back and, as a bonus, placed her left arm over his body, and the two drifted off to sleep.

The next he knew was a voice saying, "Fred, Fred, wake up, it's ten o'clock. Here is a cup of tea." On opening his eyes there was Phyllis standing by the bed fully made up and in a light overcoat and hat. She told him she had to go to London and might see him later and departed. When he fully came round and got out of bed he strolled into her living room. Phyllis had left him some breakfast and next to the plate was a key and a note. Opening the once-folded piece of paper it began:

'Dear Fred and colleague. I have been up since 7.30 and thinking about what you should do in regards to your private life. What you have been through must have been awful to bear, but I implore you to go to your wife and talk things over. Believe me, it's the best way. Anyhow it's up to you. I have left you my spare key so as to let yourself in if you want to stay. Ph.'

Not to abuse the hospitality, Freddie just freshened his face up with his hands to his face, even drying it with an unused handkerchief, then left, taking the key, just in case. He then drove to the hospital where he was told his wife had discharged herself. She was not allowed to take her baby as it was under-weight and needed special care. He then left the hospital, now knowing where to go or what to do next. His intuition told him to go to their home, saying to himself, 'if I know Deb she will want peace and quiet.'

CHAPTER 51

Stopping the car outside the still-unfurnished cottage, he approached their caravan door but instead of going straight in he slightly tapped on the door. To his surprise Deborah opened it and her first words to him were not only music to his ears but one of joy. Still in her dressing gown, she said, "Hello sweetheart, come in and hold me like you always do, that is all I want." Throwing his hat down he held her as tight as he could. Their world was back on course. She suggested they both wash and dress themselves up and go out – go out anywhere they chose. Deborah said, "Let's go to Raymead Park like we used to when you were on leave. To me that time was the best so far in my life, even though we had to part every day."

Freddie replied, "Yes, for me too." During the time since he knocked on the door, only ten minutes before, Deb never once mentioned anything about their daughter. Also he noted there were no signs of even a child expected to come home. This bothered him and made him uncomfortable but he decided until Deborah did he would act as if the child were not even in the world, let alone in the caravan. As they walked over the bridge at Boulter's Lock and into the park, the topics of conversation were the weather and of all things the Korean War. She said, "Do you think World War Three is coming Freddie?" All he could say was that he hoped not. Walking hand-in- hand just as they used to, Deborah turned, looked him in the face and said, "You have not asked me about our child, dear, why is that?" All he could say was, "After you opened the door and asked me to hold you and up 'til a moment ago you have said nothing. I left it at that, so what is happening or what has happened?"

"Well now, I have got what I always wanted – a family – and above all you dear. The baby has no appeal to me, anyway, she must stay in the hospital, she is too fragile, but I do go in and feed her twice a day," and she added, "I have named her Emma Louise, is that all right?"

"Yes, they are two lovely names. I would like to see her."

"You come then this afternoon with me."

Returning to their home prior to going to the hospital, they passed the time by going into the cottage to try and get it ready to live in. The confined space of the caravan after Wentworth was not helping matters. Then they heard a lady's voice call out, "Is anybody there?"

Both went to the door and who was stood there, none other than Phyllis. Freddie's heart began to race. Phyllis asked, "Does Mr Fred Radnor live here?"

"Yes, here he is, he's my husband."

"Could I see your identity card, sir, as I have a letter for you which I have to deliver by hand?"

"Yes, it's in my jacket, I'll get it for you." Inside Freddie was relieved that the situation was formal. Phyllis introduced herself, passing the letter over and began to leave but was invited into the caravan for a cup of tea, which she accepted. Freddie said to himself, 'if only Deborah knew!'

Phyllis and Deborah seemed to hit it off in no time, while acting the hostess. In the kitchen Freddie slipped the key into Phyllis' hand and she nodded discreetly. Deb told her what they were trying to do in the cottage but was frustrated by new planning rules and trying to get the landlord of the other three cottages to agree to the installation of electricity. Phyllis said she had a few contacts who might help. Her offer was taken up and endorsed by another cup of tea and a cigarette. Phyllis said, "Well, I must be off and let you two get on," shaking hands and saying goodbye.

Before opening the letter Freddie noticed it was addressed to a Mr & Mrs Radnor, which he thought unusual. Reading it together, they saw it was a request to come to HQ to see a certain officer. Both wondered why. But however, they both went on the appointed day and were ushered into the officer's room, accompanied by Richard who was requested to stay, which was in itself unusual. The officer began by offering the organisation's condolences over their loss and enquired how their daughter was. He then said, "As your child is in hospital, would both of you like to have a week all expenses paid in a certain hotel in Lyon, France?" And looking straight at Freddie, said that all he had to do in return was hand over some papers.

Before the officer could say another word, Deborah said, "No, but thank you all the same." As far as she was concerned she had to go to the hospital twice every day to feed their daughter, so it would help to bond to her. At one time she did not want the child and would have offered her up for adoption. "I was drifting into what they call post-natal depression. Now I want to keep her. Do you understand sir?"

The officer fully understood, continuing with small talk before shaking their hands and bidding them farewell. From there they drove to the hospital where

Deborah resumed feeding Emma. When the child was contented she fell fast asleep but before handing Emma back to the care of the nurse she invited Freddie to hold her in his arms for the first time. It was an experience which he would never forget. His face was a joy to see.

A week later little Emma was discharged from the hospital and Deborah was told the local district nurse would visit her every day at any time during the day until they were satisfied with the welfare of both mother and child. In that week prior to Emma coming home both had a lot of shopping to do for their little treasure as they called her. For one thing Deborah had to go to London to get the money to buy the items she would need, but where she went to get it no-one knew. Freddie for his part had his in the lining of his jacket. Deborah spent money on Emma including buying a Royale pram from a West End store, going to each one until they had the model she wanted. When she went out it turned heads. One nosey person enquired had she won the football pools and at this the neighbour felt the full wrath of Deborah's tongue.

Emma was now eight weeks old. One day in mid-afternoon while nursing her there was a tap, tap on the door. Still holding the child, upon opening it there stood an Indian man very smartly dressed and well groomed, about middle-aged. His first words were, "Do you happen to be a certain Mrs Deborah Churton?"

Deb's reply was, "I was once but my marriage was annulled and I am now Mrs Deborah Radnor. What is it you want?" She kept the man standing there when almost on cue Freddie came home from the technical college.

It was only then she invited the man inside. "Please sit down," and passing Emma to Freddie made some tea. "Now sir, what is your business?" He began by saying he was a distant cousin of the late Princess Devendra and her brother and that he had been appointed the executor of their estates, but could not find any legal documents and in the same breath asked Deborah could she help him in any way.

Freddie caught Deb's eye and he waved his head sideways indicating 'say no', but she ignored his advice. "Please go on, sir. If you have any more you wish to ask me."

"Thank you, I will. The solicitor in charge has been replaced by another, this time a well-known English practice and nobody can find any papers, including the wills of both victims of this tragic accident."

At this point Freddie asked him if he had any form of identification.

"Yes, I have," he answered and produced his passport and two other documents. Freddie was prepared to leave it at that when Deborah asked Freddie would he take Emma out for a walk just for a few moments as she had to tell the gentleman something in private, giving Freddie that lovely wink as she did so. Putting Emma in her pram, off he went, unaware she had given him an opportunity to 'phone Harry Carter to confirm if the man was genuine and Harry had said 'yes he is'. So Freddie told Harry why he had come and again Harry said it was he who had sent him to Deb as the last resort hoping in the same breath that he did not mind. No, he did not mind, and in any case it had nothing to do with him in any way. With that, Harry used a word he had not used since he left the army: "Good man, good man."

Freddie put down the receiver and thought to himself these army officers never change in the way they talk. When he returned, Deborah and the gentleman were outside talking. In fact they were waiting for him to return so that he could say goodbye. His parting words to them were, it was a pleasure to meet them and he placed in little Emma's hand a coin to wish her good fortune – it was above all things a gold sovereign.

Deborah lifted Emma out of her pram and said to Freddie, "Come in dear, you hold her while I make some tea and I will tell you something which until ten minutes ago was a secret. Now I have told Devendra's cousin it is a secret no longer, so you should know about it. I was going to tell you at some time, but Devendra's death has brought things forward. You see dear, when I broke down in Mogador and was sent to the hill station to convalesce, Devendra, at the suggestion of her father, accompanied me as a companion, otherwise I would have been alone except for doctors and nurses. I had met Devi a few times at parties. After a few days we both discovered we had two things in common. She had been divorced because she was barren and my marriage was a flop, a disaster, so we comforted each other and we became very close and we found comfort and happiness to the extent she was my confidante and vice versa. We shared many stories and above all some secrets. One of them was that when we got home to the UK and recovered the money and jewels we would place our share in safety deposit boxes in a West End store. We had one each, next to each other. As it turned out in my case, being what I was in stature, I had some difficulty in getting one. You had to be endorsed by two professional referees. So there you have it dear, that is where Devi's will and all her papers are. I know because she told me. She did not trust anyone else."

Freddie wanted to embrace her but was holding Emma. But when he put her down, he did so tightly and she had to plead with him to let go. He then said, "Now everything fits into place and explains it all!" So now the air was cleared and both could get on with life.

The Strand kept him on their books but seldom used him. Phyllis became a family friend as far as Deborah was concerned, but she became Freddie's mistress, as Deborah had to be careful not to conceive a child as the doctors warned her that if she did it might kill her. When they did make love, Freddie had to use a 'French letter' which neither liked.

CHAPTER 52

A year had passed and Emma was growing into a beautiful little girl. Harry had found Freddie a decommissioned chapel on a ten-year lease so he could start up in his own furniture restoration business. He would have preferred a shop but at least it would give him a start.

During this period a battle was being fought in the High Court by Devendra's Counsel over getting access to her will, which was still under lock and key. Harry Carter kept them informed about what was happening and in the meantime everything was as it stood. Jane and Tommy Haldane were still at Wentworth and eventually Deborah and Freddie moved out of the caravan into their cottage. The chapel was not to Freddie's liking and he did not wish to commit himself to a ten-year lease, so it was agreed that he would rent it – it would have to do. Meanwhile, he himself would look for a shop. Harry told him with tongue in cheek that there was a lady ghost or an apparition in the small graveyard, which was full. Freddie took no notice.

Eventually the court gave an order that the box be opened in the presence of five witnesses and so there it was, just as Deborah told them. Its contents were taken away – the whole process had taken eleven months. Emma was now in her second year and Freddie's business was not doing very well. He was insolvent on paper and kept his position at the technical college and so was with the Strand. The situation suited them. To look genuine he filled the chapel with all the junk he could find, including what Mr Brown would have burnt. In himself he knew all along from the beginning it was not what he wanted.

Deborah received a letter from Devendra's solicitor informing her that probate had been granted and would she attend the reading of Princess Devendra's will at his practice at the time and date stated. Also she could be accompanied by her husband or a friend, but they would not be allowed in his room as only beneficiaries would be allowed. It would appear that Devendra had left her something. On hearing this, Freddie made an uncharacteristic snide remark that it would be about £25. Deborah ignored his response completely as by now since he opened his business he kept drifting into melancholy. She was reluctant to ask him in case he flared up and she did not want their idyllic life, which they both had striven for, jeopardised, however small the problem. The only day he could open for business was a Saturday if he could wangle a day off from the technical college.

One such day there was nothing to do, so he put on the door 'Gone for lunch' but he had no appetite and instead went to the nearest off licence and bought a quarter bottle of whisky. He returned and sat himself on a rickety old armchair. No customer had called all day. After a few glasses and countless cigarettes he fell asleep. He was woken by the opening of the squeaky door and a voice called out, "Hello, is anyone about?"

"Yes, here I am." Looking up, it was Phyllis of all people. He offered her a drink, which she declined, but requested one of his smokes. They both lit up and Freddie poured out his problems to her. She looked around and said, "Fred, you'll never make a go of this venture. Not only are you in the wrong location but any customer who came would not take you seriously. If I were you, I would close down and forget it. But don't let me influence you. In the meantime, that chaise longue looks tempting. Come on, lock the door and I'll make you forget your troubles. I have seen it in men many times."

Freddie did not want asking twice and remarked, "I won't bother, no-one will come knocking." As it was a hot summer's day neither had much on – she just a light dress and himself shirt and trousers. Momentarily it was the complete re-enactment of that day in India when Deborah was sick in the car. This thought spurred him on. Phyllis showed him another position in which the act could be done and to him it was wonderful. Afterwards, Freddie laughed out loud and said, "There I said nobody would knock on the door," Phyllis joined him in his moment of joy and laughed with him. What he was laughing at really was that if he and Deborah had made love on that fateful day on their way home to RAF Mogador, Joan Ellison or the military police or anyone for that matter would have caught them and then what? Who knows what the consequences might have been. As far as he was concerned, it did not bear thinking about.

Both made themselves look respectable and left hand in hand. Here he thought he had found a true friend, someone he could trust and confide in. In fact just as they parted Freddie said so and Phyllis' reply was, "Yes, that would be wonderful." He gently kissed her on the mouth, then they went their different ways.

On arriving home, Deborah asked him if he had had many customers.

"Yes, just one, a lady, but she didn't buy anything but we talked about things in general. She was very well dressed and smart. She was quite taken by me and she would tell her friends where I was and what I could do."

"Oh well that's all right then."

CHAPTER 53

The day came when Deborah had to go to the solicitor's office to hear Devendra's will being read. There were three other beneficiaries. Freddie concluded they also had been left something. After about half an hour the office door opened in a state of panic. It seems Deborah had fainted. Freddie rushed in to her and asked for a glass of water and she gradually came round.

Before they left the solicitor gave Freddie an envelope. When he looked at it, it was addressed to 'Aircraftsman F.W. Radnor'. He put it in his pocket unopened. When they got back home, picking up Emma on the way, they both sat down to tea and Deborah told him that she fainted because Devi had left her £10,000 and some jewellery. Freddie thought, 'now what? Will this change our lives?' And his prophetic thoughts would come true to the letter. Deborah felt like celebrating and asked Freddie would he drive into town and buy a bottle of champagne. He did so willingly as it gave him an opportunity to read this formally-addressed letter alone. On opening it he read it.

After he opened and read the letter he was in a semi-state of shock and handed it to Deborah to read for herself. Halfway through it, tears flowed down her face and on finishing she burst into not only a full cry but a howling out. Emma in her innocence followed suit. As for Freddie he was dumbstruck. Both embraced for a moment. Deborah said to him, "I must hold Emma to stop her crying."

"Whisky?" he said to her.

"Yes please, dear, and a cigarette." After ten minutes Deborah said "We must take Emma to my mother for a few days, both of us need some time to be quiet and have no distractions so we can take all of this in."

Freddie agreed, so the champagne remained unopened. Freddie went out for a walk while Deb put Emma down for the night. When she returned it was near bedtime. Both were quiet, both retired knowing their life together was on a knife edge. The champagne remained unopened – there was nothing to celebrate. Devendra's vindictive letter had put a stop to that. On retiring to bed they both tried in vain to sleep but to no avail. What could she do? She tried to sooth him by indicating she wanted to make love but Freddie said on lighting his bedside candle, "The best thing to do is talk things through."

He began, "You do realise, don't you, you are now rich?"

"Yes I do dear and I'm going to give you half. It's only right." At this he began to raise his voice but she stopped him in his tracks by putting her hand over his mouth. Then she got out of bed. When she returned Freddie was fast asleep, his right arm on Deb's pillow. Somehow she wriggled in beside him and she too went off to sleep. They were woken by Emma crying. It was 6.30. Their treasure wanted her breakfast. She told him to stay there until he wanted to get up. At breakfast she put in front of him her plan as to what to do. First she would seek advice from her bank manager as this money would now come to the attention of the Inland Revenue. Freddie nodded in approval.

"What are your plans for today?" she enquired.

"I don't know. I'll probably go to the college," and left it at that. But he did know. In himself it would be the Strand. They said goodbye, see you later, Freddie giving her a tug and a less-than-warm kiss on her cheek, which Deborah noticed. It was just a matter of fact. Freddie did go to the Strand and let it be known to them that if he was required he would like to go out in the field. At this request they were surprised. When they asked him why his reply was he preferred it. In the meantime he was told to carry on at the technical college. In himself he left the building feeling a bit more superior, as if to match Deborah's inheritance of all that money.

When he returned home Deborah gave him a warm welcome and had cooked him his favourite meal. She said she had had a wonderful day and after she put Emma to bed told him what she had done. First she went to her bank and prepared to set up a trust fund of £5,000 for Emma to mature when she was twenty-one. And as for herself, she would look for a bigger house with all modern furniture, a nice big kitchen and a garden for all three of them. All he said was, "Well dear it is your money. You go ahead and do what you want. I will just follow." She also said that when Emma was sitting on her lap in the bank manager's office he came round from his desk to pick her up but she cried very loudly and he had to give her back to me.

At this point Freddie said, "Have you noticed that when you give her over to me she does the same? She will not let me nurse or cuddle her."

"Yes I have. It seems she does not like men, but she will grow out of it. In the meantime let us enjoy our good fortune. Heaven knows we have earned it one way or another." This remark unexpectedly lifted his mood.

On retiring to bed he reminded her that she should take up driving lessons and buy a car for herself. He said there was nothing like it – it gave you complete freedom and independence. Deborah saw his point and bearing in mind she had to be careful she indicated she wanted him. Afterwards they flopped off to sleep. Now the deep love they found in India had rekindled.

But there was a fly in the ointment. She was not happy with his decision to take on a higher level of duties which would take him away for days on end, but to keep him she had to go along with what he had decided to do. She wished he could have made a success of his business and as for that the chapel, or Radnor's Renovations as he called it, it remained closed.

One Friday when he came home from the technical college he opened his wallet and gave Deborah £8. She asked him why and said it was not necessary. Freddie's face became red and flushed, it was a sign he was trying to control himself. He told her it was for housekeeping money and was it enough? And from now on he would give it to her once a month as he was now on salary. At this Deborah said, "Why, why, it is not necessary." He retorted that it was his duty as a husband but above everything else he did not want to live off bloody Devendra's money and at this time and moment in this our home our lives would remain the same, continuing, "That bitch has come between us from the grave." He ended his outburst with, "There is something wrong here, something I can't put my finger on, but one day I will," and it was left at that.

Deborah's response was one of silent shock and she turned on every charm in the book. She had no choice, she was in a dilemma.

After turning things over in her mind all the following week she started to cry and Deborah shouted out, "Oh that bloody child she never seems to stop. I don't know why." At this Freddie stormed out and spent the night with Phyllis.

CHAPTER 54

The next day while at the college he received by hand a message to report to HQ without delay. When he arrived he was told to go home, pack enough things for a week, then report back for orders. When he reached home the place was desolate but he had no time to find out why. He packed his bag and returned to HQ where he was told about his mission.

"Tonight Fred you will be flown to Paris. There you will be met in the usual way, then introduced to Cecile who is one of our agents. She is a very attractive high-class prostitute. From there you both travel to this railway station on the French-Belgian border. At this small country station is a Gladstone bag like this one which has been put in the left luggage office by one of our men for safe keeping, but the retrieving ticket has been damaged. All we have are the first two numbers of the ticket, but the man in charge of the office won't give the bag over. He said he must have the complete ticket or identify in detail its contents. We must get this bag. The other side wants it as well. We have had three attempts but each one has failed. So see if you can retrieve it for us. It's very important. We think the girl might be a distraction if you come up with something. The ruse is that you are Pilot Officer Defton-Childe on honeymoon. Your wife has her marriage certificate and hidden in her luggage is all the money you need. How about it?"

Freddie agreed and off he went. When he met Cecile he was turned over by her beauty. She turned heads just like Deborah used to and they set off on the train journey to the small quaint town, booked into a hotel to wait and come up with a plan. While on the train, Freddie had already come to the conclusion that they would attract much attention walking about a small town as a couple. He told Cecile and said to her:

"You get off at the station, book into the hotel alone and I will go on to the next station and leave it there. Then I will make my way back to the hotel and take a separate room. What we have to do is look over the left luggage office to find a weak spot which we can exploit." It seemed after two days it would be difficult, then on one visit he noticed that in order to get a larger sized box into the place a large door had to be opened. This was the way in, so between them they looked around the town for a large box. Cecile found one and they filled it with anything they could get their hands on. They then got it to the station where Freddie asked the attendant if he could leave it there for about three days. Cecile would volunteer out of the blue to act as an interpreter then, while the large door was open and she turned on her charms, Freddie slipped in with the identical bag and swapped it for the one they wanted. The bag was put into the large box and Freddie returned two days later to collect it with the genuine ticket, all the time Cecile was chatting up the attendant.

The plan worked and the bag was retrieved and taken to the British Embassy in Paris. Mission completed! Freddie said to Cecile he would like to stay in Paris for a few days and would she show him around as when he was there before it had not been a happy time. She said she would be delighted and over four days they went out on the city. Cecile invited Freddie to stay in her personal apartment, not the one where she entertained her clients. Of course he accepted. Just like when he went to Limoges to meet and bring Deborah home from her exile.

On the second night Cecile after visiting the Folies Bergère, Cecile took a bath prior to retiring to bed. Freddie had one too and as he emerged from the bathroom Cecile invited him into her bed, saying to him, "This is different – from my heart to you." It was just like Phyllis in Maidenhead!
'My, my,' he thought, 'these ladies of pleasure have a heart of gold.'

It was now time for both to say goodbye. Cecile said she had to visit a rich client. In himself he wished she did not have to but it was her chosen profession. When they parted she gave him a kiss to remember, adding, "Look me up if you should be in Paris anytime." He could do no more than say, "The same goes for you, if you come to England."

CHAPTER 55

Freddie arrived at Northolt still as Pilot Officer Defton-Childe and was put up overnight in the officers' quarters and the next day he would resume his true identity and undergo a de-briefing at HQ. Well, if nothing else, he could always say if he was asked what he did that he was – 'an RAF officer', that might open a few doors!

That evening all the trappings of being an officer were still there. At HQ he was ushered in to be debriefed by none other than the Chief himself. He was congratulated on his success and told, "The retrieved bag was very useful to us. How did you do it where three other attempts had already failed?" When he told them, once more congratulations were forthcoming. He was offered a drink and a cigarette and was told that he would be put on the reserve list as his cover had been exposed thanks to his wife's indiscretion at a party and also that she was in semi-custody until he saw her. Also, his daughter Emma was a 'ward of court' and the child was being cared for by his in-laws.

"I am so sorry Radnor, but that is how things are. It is up to you what happens next. Your wife can be released at once if you so wish and you take responsibility for her." He was shocked but not surprised and said he would take care of her. Freddie was given a large envelope and told to return to the technical college until things settled down. He could do no more but nod in agreement.

He collected his treasured Humber and drove to where Deborah was being cared for. To him it was a 'safe house'. However, there were things in certain places which gave its purpose away. He was greeted by a smartly dressed woman who, on shaking his hand said, "Your wife has been told you are on your way to take her home, sir. She has been very quiet and has hardly said a word to anyone."

He replied that he understood. Deborah then appeared through a door disguised as a bookshelf. He did no more when he saw her but open his arms. She rushed over to him and as he closed his arms around her she said, "Hold me Freddie, hold me." Freddie had lost count of the times in their lives she had said those words. As he drove along neither had any idea or thoughts as to their destination, no words were spoken. The silence was becoming unbearable to both of them, but what to say? Suddenly Deborah said, "Freddie pull over, I have an idea."

He did so and asked her, "What now?"

She said, "Let us put back the clock to when I left you at Maidenhead that Saturday afternoon. Look, Maidenhead is just up the road. Stop the Humber near the Bear Hotel."

"OK, why, do you want a drink?"

"No, just do as I say."

"Oh, very well."

When they got to the Bear she said, "You go in to the same bar and wait for me. Buy two drinks and I will come in as though it is two o'clock on that Saturday." Reluctantly he went along with this charade. He thought she was going to run away but no, in she came and word for word said to him, "I'm sorry I'm late, sweetheart." They drank up and made their way to the café, then she got out of her seat and said, "Goodbye, darling, goodbye. I must catch my train, then in ten minutes you go to the station as you did to go home."

Once more, "All right," Freddie said, "but I don't see the point."

"Just do as I say dear, it might just work." He remembered the route he had taken and arrived at the station. Deborah was nowhere to be seen. He then went over the bridge to the platform and waited. It was at this point he realised what she was up to. He sensed someone was watching him. As the train stopped a voice called out, "Freddie, don't go, don't go. I am not going to Germany with Maurice, I want to be with you," and she came running down the steps straight into his arms. She said, "Sod the lot of them, let us run off to anywhere." As the train pulled away she said, "That is what I should have done. I curse myself for not doing it. Would you have come with me Freddie, would you?"

He said, "Yes, I think I would and tonight we will put up in a hotel and decide where and what we will do. But before tomorrow morning comes we will be in bed with nothing on and we will be exhausted by breakfast time, which we won't bother about. It will be a night to remember till the day we die." And then they left for a hotel wherever one might be.

During what was left of the day and booking into a hotel, they went out for dinner and then to a dance hall but both were restless and returned to the hotel telling the night porter that they wished not to be disturbed as they had just got married. With a smile he understood and nodded his head and the rest of the night was theirs. They booked out mid-morning and had to decide what to do next, so Freddie suggested they go to Raymead Park and talk. Deborah agreed. Sitting on a park seat Freddie decided to call the shots and looking at her radiant face said, "We have to make up our minds what we are going to do from today and whatever we decide it must be for the rest of our lives."

Deborah said, "Yes, we must, we cannot go on like this." So Freddie retrieved a penny from his pocket and tossed it in the air for who speaks first. Deborah said 'tails' and tails it was. Holding his hand she said she did not want any more to do with Emma, "As I don't like being a mother. There is no problem as Emma is with her grandmother and the child is happier and content with her. Let us hope Mum makes a better job of bringing her up than she did of me." Freddie went to interrupt but she put up her hand as if to say I won the toss. She then said for the time being she would withdraw her large house from the market.

"I want to live there, do you understand dear? You can give me the house-keeping money like every husband does." Freddie nodded his head. It seemed it was she who was calling the shots, not him. She ended by saying "Freddie, you are a good carpenter and joiner but you are no businessman, you leave that side to me. Anyway, we won't go bust with all the loot from India. All I want is to be with you, always. Well what do you say dear?"

Freddie could find no words. Inwardly, that is what he had always wanted. He then said, "Well Deb, if you had called out to me on that fateful Saturday, I would not have become an agent or spy as I would not have got into the train compartment and picked up the discarded newspaper and recognised Ginger and solved the robbery at Maggadore. It was he who told me and the Strand who was behind the whole thing, but it is water under the bridge. Let us forget it all and start afresh."

They both got up from the park seat and walked hand-in-hand towards the small bridge overlooking Boulter's Lock entrance and they drove back along the Bath Road to Deborah's house. As they entered the place was cold and musty but together they soon put that right. Among some mail that had been delivered over her absence was one addressed to her. She opened it and it was from the Home Office ordering her to attend a disciplinary hearing regarding the Official Secrets Act which she had signed. She showed it to Freddie who said, whether true or not, it would be all right. But Deb was less convinced. It had put a damper on their lovely few days.

Inwardly Freddie too was uneasy but did not show it. Before a day and time was arranged, Freddie while out in Maidenhead was approached by a man he had not seen before and who told him, "We understand your position Fred but don't worry. At the enquiry they will only go through the motions and nothing will happen to your wife. But, in return in an emergency, could we use your shop and home if only for one night?"

Freddie knew that if he said no they would throw the book at Deborah so he said, "Yes, that's all right by me." The man shook his hand and on departing said, "Good chap."

They attended the enquiry and they made it look serious but it was a charade. As they left Deb remarked, "That was close, wasn't it dear?

Freddie said, "Yes they are not a bad lot." When they were back home he told her the full story. She flew into a rage but this time it was his turn. All he said was, "Well what would you prefer, my arrangement or you standing trial for breaking the Secrets Act and five or more years in Holloway Prison, because that is what you would get!"

She had no answer. She knew it was the second time that he had saved her from prison – the other time was of course in Maggadore. She broke into tears and went into his arms once more. Deborah suddenly broke away and asked him what happened to the ruby and gold necklace he took from her handbag. He said he still had it but only he knew where it was and it was safe.

EPILOGUE

For the next twenty or more years nothing dramatic happened. They both settled into a domestic routine. The Strand, as Freddie still called it, used the rooms and rented out to them. They always knew when they were shielding or hiding someone, it was as if Deborah's house was cut in two. This now happy couple were never bothered, except by a monthly money order in payment. One Wednesday, when they always closed the shop, they decided to have a day at Kempton Park races. Freddie was dressed first and he got the Humber from the garage. Deb was upstairs getting herself made up. To him she was taking too long and he called up to her to hurry or they would miss the first race. She shouted down, "Just a few more minutes, dear." He in turn said, "I'll be in the car, you lock up."

"OK," she said, "I will." Deborah locked the front door and on reaching the car Freddie was slumped on the seat, his hands on the steering wheel. He was motionless and she could not do anything. She ran back inside the house to 'phone for an ambulance or the police or even their doctor. She did not scream or call out on the way. She was dumbstruck.

The next morning the milkman on his rounds called in to deliver his usual order. As he got to the front door it was half open, which to him was suspicious. A cat ran out as he put the bottles down. He called out but got no reply. To him something was not right. Then his attention was drawn to the car and he went over to it. When he opened the car door inside were two bodies who he immediately recognised as Mr & Mrs Radnor. They were both dead. Shocked, he went into the house and 'phoned the police and said what he had found. They ordered him to stay there until they arrived and to touch nothing. He could do no more than obey.

    The first on the scene were the local police but within the hour the place was swarming with Special Branch, a government pathologist and of course the Strand. Among all of these a supremo was appointed. Up until then nothing had been moved. In turn the head of each section was allowed to look into the Humber Snipe to see for themselves, but only look. What each one saw was a male in the driver's seat dressed in a blazer, an RAF blue shirt and an RAF tie. On his hands was a pair of leather driving gloves. Sat by his side was a beautiful lady with long blonde hair, so close to the man you could not put the cigarette paper between them. Her right arm was placed under the man's lower back and her head rested at a tilt on his shoulder, but with vomit and blood dripping from her lips. To all present it was nothing, but of course Deborah had staged an exact replay of the time she was sick and Freddie had wiped her clean on the way back to RAF Maggadore. So their life span ended as it had all began. All because of a simple everyday order from the driver's superior officer to be the driver of Wing Commander Churton.

POSTSCRIPT

When Deborah ran into the house it was not to 'phone anyone. She knew what she wanted and had to do. By the evidence on her writing desk, it was to write a note to her parents and to Emma, also to the police and as a postscript 'to whom it may concern'. This last was commandeered by the Coroner, in spite of protests by Special Branch, and the Strand, but the Coroner won the day. The inquest was opened and adjourned for two weeks for the autopsy on both the bodies. The Coroner came to the verdict in regards Frederick William Radnor that death was by natural causes – heart failure. But Mrs Deborah Radnor needed further investigation. Freddie had made a will leaving what was in his name to his son, Frederick and to his friend, Denise, residing in France. Their address was on the will. It surprised everyone.

Everything regarding Deborah was difficult; no will could be found; all she left was a clutch of letters sealed down. All were written in the space of about an hour after she discovered her Freddie slumped over the car seat. At her inquest the Coroner recorded the verdict of 'she died by cyanide poisoning whilst the balance of her mind was disturbed'. The Coroner released the two bodies to be buried side-by-side as she had wished in one of the letters.

Frederick and Denise made the arrangements and at the reception afterwards it was discovered that when Deborah had left the convent and surfaced in the town near Limoges, the ex-members of the Resistance thought and convinced themselves that she was the missing SOE agent who during 1944 had descended from an aircraft into their unit and made her a hero. That was the only reason she had sent for Freddie – to fetch her through her friend and lover Devendra.

Probate was granted to Deborah's assets and was included in Freddie's will as he would have been the recipient if Deborah had died first. One of the letters not written by her but by one Lt Colonel Hontas dated 1960, in which he stated that he knew Aircraftsman Radnor had removed the ruby and gold necklace because at the reception it was planted in her handbag so that they would have evidence to convict her of smuggling but they had not banked on her being ill on the way back to Maggadore. Anyway the necklace was a fake and worth nothing. It remained in Freddie's toolbox until it was destroyed in a fire.